Fata
Morgana

WILLIAM
KOTZWINKLE

FATA
MORGANA

Marlowe & Company

First Marlowe edition 1996

Published by
Marlowe & Company
632 Broadway, Seventh Floor
New York, NY 10012

Copyright © 1977,1996 by William Kotzwinkle
Illustrations Copyright © 1977, 1996 by Joe Servello

Printed in the United States of America

Library of Congress Catalog Card Number: 96-76840

ISBN: 1-56924-787-0

For Inspector L.

THE INCIDENTS that follow were suggested
by an article written by Madame Blavatsky
in the *Spiritual Scientist* for November
1875. Mme Blavatsky received the details of
the story from the Adept known as Hillarion,
sometimes called Hillarion Smerdis. Endrei-
nek Agardi of Koloswar considered some of
the facts erroneously detailed. Anyone caring
to visit the police archives in Paris will find the
entire incident hotly denied. Where the
truth of the matter lies will perhaps never be
known. The present account is but one of
many, and while it is faithful in some respects
to the original tales, it sought its own
course and resolution. One can only say that
to each of us Fata Morgana reveals a different
part of its restless, shimmering nature.

PARIS, 1861

T H E faces in the crowd were dark, from Spain, Morocco, Constantinople, and a sensuous air prevailed, exotic and violent. The shops were filled with cheap merchandise; a dark-haired prostitute stood on the corner, smiling, and Inspector Picard passed her, making his way through Pigalle.

Glancing at his watch, he quickened his step, muttering the usual nonsense to himself about eating less and training more, for he was breathing heavily from his exertion.

Yet he moved more swiftly than any other on the busy street, with the surprising swiftness of the bear who has suddenly found reason to move. And like the bear he had a heavy, natural grace, despite his fifty-two years and the extra pounds around his waistline, produced by a particularly delicious lemon tart sold on the rue Dauphine; he longed for one now, for as always when on the scent, a strange hunger stole over him—he felt he could devour Baron Mantes alive, swallow him down and munch his bones.

As he hurried along, Picard studied certain faces carefully, taking note of their eyes, and also of their hands—the way they handled a franc note, almost caressing it, ritually folding it and slipping it away—these were men he would see again, in the intimate embrace of arrest, or they would find their fate elsewhere, or they would escape absolutely. The city was vast, sprawling, who could know it all?

He left the street of cheap pimps and prostitutes, entering the chausée d'Antin, where the Great Whores had their apartments. The carriages at the curb belonged to diplomats, ambassadors, and the voices he heard were discreet, refined. Nonetheless, last month he'd assisted in the removal of a body from one of the luxurious gardens, where a duel had been fought over a whore's favor. Madness prevailed everywhere.

Ahead he saw the lights of the Opéra. The street was lined with waiting carriages. Among them he spotted Paradis the ragman, a wicker basket over his shoulder, a filthy paper flower in his lapel. Picard approached the informer quickly. "He's still here?"

"The box seats," said Paradis, staring wildly around him.

Picard handed him a roll of franc notes. "Stay and point him out to me."

Paradis hurriedly thrust the money in his pocket and shuffled off as fast as he could, his enormous shoes slapping in the mud, his baggy pants trailing over his heels. Picard watched the retreating ragman for a moment, then turned and walked into the lobby of the theatre as the final ovation was being offered the horned and embattled singers.

He took his position where he could observe those music lovers who'd held box seats. The crowd filed past, involved in the usual flirtations, the regular boredom. All they'd killed was another evening. There was no butchery in their eyes. Picard waited—Baron Mantes will carry himself in a special way, for the training of a Berlin fencing master cannot be erased from the body.

Those from the box seats were now descending the staircase—the noblest faces in the Empire. Among them were numerous men who walked with the authority of polished swordsmen, but only one glanced about him with cautious watching eyes, even while his lips smiled softly at the young woman beside him, and his gaze instinctively met Picard's. The Inspector stood on tiptoe, stared past the man, calling, "Here, Yvette, here I am! Where is little Charles?" then plunged into the crowd, keeping the tall blond head of his quarry in view. Baron Mantes was accompanying a young woman in white, whose gown was trimmed with undulating bands of black satin, a touch of death upon her already. If you knew, mademoiselle, with whom you walk . . .

Picard tried to close in, but the Baron was in control of the situation, scanning the crowd with the nervous tension of a man-at-arms. Picard's hand was resting inside his jacket, upon the handle of his revolver, but to draw it here, to attempt arrest in this crowd, would endanger many lives.

He followed the Baron into the street; Mantes was already showing the young woman into a waiting carriage and quickly followed her, closing the door behind him. Picard hurried among the other carriages, gaining an advantage in the crowded muddy street, for the horses were slow to move out, and he found an unoccupied carriage.

"Driver, do you see that coach, three ahead of us, a young woman's face at the window?" Picard held his badge out and the driver, a hawk-nosed black-bearded fellow, glanced at it and moved his eyes in the direction Picard indicated.

"Yes, I see her."

"If you lose sight of her tonight, she is certain to die at the hands of the man who is with her." Picard climbed into the carriage, and the driver swiftly maneuvered into the main line of traffic.

Picard lowered his window. "He mustn't know we're following him."

"He'll know nothing," snapped the black-bearded driver, his eyes fixed on the Baron's carriage, and Picard knew he'd chosen one of those carriage men who will drive you into hell if you request it.

The street was filled with opera lovers, and they stepped haughtily in front of the hawk's carriage. "Out of my way!" he snarled, cracking his whip and moving so close to the terrified pedestrians his carriage wheel went over the edge of a woman's long trailing skirt.

They continued along the avenue de l'Opéra, keeping steadily behind the Baron's vehicle; Picard saw the young woman's beautiful head at the window. The last woman the Baron had escorted had also been beautiful. She was found in a bedroom of the Hôtel du Rhin, her eyes open and a sheet tucked up to her neck. As the bedcovers were in a state of dishevelment, only when they were taken away was it discovered that the rest of her body was not in the bed.

Picard's stomach growled; he was ravenously hungry. Withdrawing his revolver from inside his jacket, he opened the cartridge gate, clicking it nervously, then cocked the hammer and lowered it again. The carriages turned onto the rue de Rivoli. He rapped on the sliding panel in front of him, which quickly opened.

"When his carriage stops, make note of the address and drive me on past it one block. Then you must hurry to the Prefecture and explain that Baron Mantes has been found. Tell them Picard sent you."

"Your man is turning again."

Picard leaned toward the window, studying the momentary profile of his quarry as the lead carriage moved into the rue des Archives. Mantes was himself glancing out the window, watching the traffic that followed him.

"He's stopping. Shall I turn? The street is narrow . . ."

"Cross the intersection . . . straight . . . stop now . . ." Picard jumped down on the blind side of the carriage and hurried to the corner building. Removing his top hat, he placed his nose on the cold brick, and slowly swiveled his head so that one eye only was cast down the street where the Baron and the young woman were descending from the carriage. A flower seller's awning marked the center of the block and they passed beside it, through an adjacent doorway.

Picard signaled his driver to move on, and walked round the corner, toward the flower seller's stall. There were but a few fresh bouquets; dried flowers of the season filled the shelves and rustled softly in the autumn breeze as Picard passed, entering the building. The hallway was empty and dim. He climbed the stairs quickly. As he turned the landing, he encountered a middle-aged woman, fat, menacing, seated behind her counter—the concierge. She was opening her large mouth, but closed it as Picard showed his shield, at the same time bringing one finger to his lips.

The smell of a fine dinner came from the open door behind the woman, momentarily beguiling Picard. He saw her dining table; she'd arranged her apartment and her life so that she could watch all movements in her house. She watched now, as Picard stepped directly up to her and whispered, "In what room is the couple who just entered?"

"At the head of the staircase, monsieur. Number 31."

He climbed the next flight, glad for the rug that muffled his steps, and stopped in the hall outside number 31. All was quiet within. He lowered his shoulder and charged the door. The hinges groaned, the old dried frame split apart and the door crashed onto the floor ahead of him as he thundered into the room. The shock of the collision slowed him slightly; Baron Mantes spun around, shattering the gas lamp with his cane.

Drawing his revolver in the darkness, Picard fired at the shadowy figure, heard the bullet splinter a mirror across the room. Then, in a sudden burst of firelight, the Baron's cane appeared, hissing toward his head. Unable to escape it, he saw with frozen clarity each detail of the approaching cane, handle shaped into a ball and claw, the iron ball crashing against his skull, driving him to his knees.

Blood ran into his eyes. The Baron's white shirt cuff appeared, his jeweled studs gleaming as Picard rolled, the iron cane whipping past his head again, missing him by a hair's-breadth. The room was burning, the oil of the shattered gas lamp spreading across the rug, and he saw the young woman's terrified face beyond the leaping flames.

"Run!" growled Picard, and she ran, across the flaming rug, to the open doorway. He heard the crisply starched linen of the Baron's sleeve, smelled the elegant killer's cologne, received the solid-iron cane across his throat. He fell backward, firing blind, gasping for air; the grinning lunatic charged with mad fury in his eyes. Picard squeezed off four rounds, saw them go wide of the Baron's lightning-fast shadow, and the fencing master's cane struck again, tearing the pistol from Picard's hand before the final round could be fired.

Picard stumbled onto the hearth of the fireplace, crashing into the fire tools. He hurled an iron shovel at the Baron, who parried and drove it across the room without missing a step of his advance upon Picard. The cane lashed out, clearing the mantelpiece of its figurines as Picard ducked low and charged with a heavy iron fire tongs in his hand, driving it into the Baron's ribs. The madman's momentum was stopped. Picard sought the offensive, swung the fire tongs against the Baron's cheek, laying open a long bloody gash, but the Baron smiled, blood trickling down his chin, and renewed his charge.

Iron mastery rang out against Picard. He swung the

fire tongs desperately, his forearms knotting with pain as he beat off the Baron's blows. The iron weapons met in the air, their black shafts crossing; the Baron's cane found its way between the two arms of the tongs, and he twisted his weapon savagely, wrenching the tongs from Picard's grip.

The Inspector saw the ball and claw once again, briefly, as it landed above the bridge of his nose. Then he was lost in unconsciousness, chasing the Baron across a dream Paris, a Paris that had become smoke-filled, through which he fought to find his way.

He woke upon the floor, in an inferno. The Baron had fled the flames, and Picard rose, struggling through them toward the door. Blazing wood crashed around him as he stumbled into the hall, into an impenetrable curtain of smoke. He groped in the smoke, feeling his way along the red-hot walls, his eyes and nose burning, his throat constricted, his heart suffocating.

The skin of the wall peeled away, then collapsed, revealing the flames that were devouring the entire floor. He lurched through the smoke, trying not to breathe, but forced to inhale the raging cloud. The flames leapt up—the staircase fell away before his eyes, leaving only a flaming hole before him. The landing creaked beneath him, and the soles of his shoes were melting with the heat. Through the crackling of the flames, he heard a hideous wailing. He ran toward it, through another fiery doorway, into another dying room. There was no air, only smoke, and his lungs were bursting in his chest. The wailing cry drew him blindly through the room. He fell in the smoke and crawled across the floor like an infant, his heart pounding wildly. His hand touched the wall and he heard the high-pitched scream directly above him. Reaching up, he clutched a windowsill and raised himself.

The lights of Paris were just beyond him, winking through the deadly grey curtain. He tucked the howling house cat under his arm and threw himself against the window.

"P A U L . . . Paul . . . wake up . . ."

He didn't wish to wake. Memories of a burning desert assailed him and he believed it was Algeria and that the long-dead campaign in which he'd served was still on. The soldiers were singing in his brain, singing of old General Bugeaud, who'd forgotten to put his helmet on during a surprise attack:

> Have you seen the helmet, the helmet,
> Have you seen the helmet of old man Bugeaud?

The old man led the troops bareheaded into battle, and Picard followed him, across a burning desert. His own helmet was lost, and enemy muskets were firing bullets into his brain. The pain was intense and he didn't want to wake.

"Paul . . ."

He opened his eyes, saw a doctor, and an old army comrade. The doctor was listening to his heart. His comrade, Albert the thief, tapped him on the cheek.

"Keep your eyes open."

He struggled to raise himself. Serrated knives ran across his brow, slicing his brain, turning Albert's lean-boned face into a rippling pattern of light. Picard fought against the pain and swung his legs to the side of the bed.

"No, monsieur, you must not get up!"

"Albert, help me out of here . . ."

"Gentlemen, I implore you . . ."

He gathered his strength and stepped to the floor. "What happened, Albert? I remember the window . . ."

"You fell through it. A lovely drop. The awning saved you. They removed you from a mountain of flowers."

"Monsieur Picard, you were nearly asphyxiated. Recovery from this sort of thing is long and very difficult. The after-effects . . ."

"Please, Doctor," said Picard, struggling to keep himself conscious. "A little knowledge is a dangerous thing."

The room spun as he dressed in his evening clothes. He adjusted his top hat over the bandage that had been wrapped around his temples. "I had gloves."

"Of course." Albert handed them to him.

Picard attempted a bow to the doctor. "My thanks to you."

"You're a fool, monsieur."

"Albert, do you remember the little song . . ." He struggled to keep his stomach down, for it had begun to rise and fall in a violent storm. They entered the hallway of the hospital. "Do you remember, we sang it in Algeria . . ."

"Which song? Or shall we sing them all?"

Picard leaned on his friend, and they walked through the lobby of the hospital, singing,

"Have you seen the helmet, the helmet,
Have you seen the helmet of old man Bugeaud . . ."

The sun struck Picard as they entered the street, the muted autumn light as blinding as the desert sun. He closed his eyes, fire leaping in his head, pain mounting at the base of his skull.

"Some easy pickings on this street," said Albert, glancing at the storefronts. "Small jobs, but they keep one's fingers toned up."

Picard stumbled forward; he didn't recognize the street, the shops, didn't care, his head was going to explode. Albert touched his sleeve, nodded toward a cloud of pink chiffon coming from a doorway. There were ruffles, a turban of twined scarlet, a fringe of auburn hair along the girl's forehead. Picard tried to focus as she entered her carriage. The vision in his left eye was disturbed by the swelling there; he saw only a blur of crinolines, the turning of a tiny yellow shoe . . .

"She's just come from her dressmaker," said Albert, pausing to investigate through the shopwindow. "I don't like cracking places like these, especially at night. Too many rolls of satin and lace all around you in the dark, you feel like you're lost in somebody's underwear."

The shop was a riot of fabric—flowered muslins, brocade, crêpe de Chine sewn with gold and silver stars. Picard felt feverish, heard himself babbling of cashmeres, taffeta, anything, to trick himself into thinking he was

well. "I grew up next door to a dressmaker . . . spent my
childhood peeking through a keyhole. The ladies . . . undressing . . ."

"A blessed childhood," said Albert.

"Yes . . . I saw wonderful things each day . . ."

"Marie-Rose, Marie-Thérèse . . ."

"An endless stream of beauty . . ."

". . . Yvette, Denise . . ."

"I floated in that stream . . ."

". . . Jeanette, Paulette, Lucy . . ." Albert named the
names of women, like beads on a rosary. Picard stared
through the dressmaker's window, caught sight of a chemi-
sette, tossed over the edge of a lacquered dressing screen.
His battered spirit moved faintly, quickening, as a blue
silk garter followed, and the owner of the shop snatched
her curtains shut. Picard turned, they walked. "There was
one lady from my childhood, Albert. I can still see her. I
am at the keyhole, she is bending over. A deep wide-open
neck . . . trimmed with ribbons . . ."

". . . and her tits . . ."

"Like . . . nothing that can be imagined. At eight years
of age such things . . ."

"I'm ashamed to admit," said Albert, leading them on
down the street, "that my great memories—you know,
the memories that stick in the heart like these tits you
speak of—are all of robberies I committed. There was
not even the rustle of my coat, nor the slightest breath.
I was invisible. I search for such moments on every job,
but they don't always come. One is not always worthy
of the God of Thieves." He reached in his pocket, brought
out a thin cigar. "But I've planned a new job . . . a great
work of crime. I've decided to . . ." He struck a match to

the cigar. ". . . steal the piece of the True Cross from the bedside of the Emperor. It rests there, in a tiny casket, between two hollow sapphires. You've heard of it? No? It was found on a chain around the neck of Charlemagne. I have an interested buyer. It is, of course . . ." He tossed the match away. ". . . the Pope."

They walked slowly, toward the Seine. Picard kept his good eye open. In the distance were other floating clouds of silk and velvet, and parasols twirling in the autumn sunlight along the river's edge.

H E sat staring at the shabby wallpaper of his room. Two weeks in bed is enough to ruin a man. He turned toward the window, saw the young men again, in the building across the way. They were standing on their balcony, looking down at the rue de Nesle, and beyond it, toward Dauphine. Young hustlers of the Quarter. Figuring how to swindle a few francs this fine evening, and how to spend it.

They turned, left the balcony windows open. The November wind blew the curtains. He watched them leave the room. They're going lightly down the stairs now. The one with the beer belly will fart like a wild horse when he hits the street, and his pal will smile at the daughter of the concierge. I know what they'll do; I watch from my window. Picard has turned into an old woman, keeps track of everything on the rue de Nesle. I used to break wine bottles over my head. For a joke. Now I sit here . . . like a turnip.

He rose from his old leather armchair; he'd worn numerous holes in it, which were carefully stitched with cobbler's thread. The chair had many scars, like its owner, and he'd always been comfortable in it.

He reeled toward the kitchen, knocked dizzily about, his head pounding with pain.

How can I report to the Prefect in such condition?

He sliced some bread, took a dirty plate from the pile of dishes, pistols, and ammunition that covered his kitchen counter. The pistols were his favorites—a Colt .358 and the breech-loading Lefaucheux. Between them, guarded by their black barrels, was the gold snuffbox given him by Prince Vatra, a little reward for a private job. A detective can do well for himself in Paris if he's efficient and discreet; the young woman who'd threatened the Prince with blackmail had been persuaded to desist, the six-and-a-half-inch barrel of the Lefaucheux held between her eyes on a dark night, in a narrow street. She was in Amsterdam now, repairing her jangled nerves.

He picked up the Colt; his hand trembled uncontrollably, and the far wall at which he aimed was made of rubber, swaying and bending in a sickening dance.

A sudden knock on the door spun him around like a thief in hiding.

"Who is it?"

"Bissonette."

Picard uncocked his pistol, unlocked the door. Inspector Bissonette touched the edge of his hat in a drunken little salute, as Picard's heart sank.

The ruined old detective smiled at Picard in his pajamas, and emitted an absinthe-soaked cloud toward him as he spoke. "How are you feeling?"

"All right," said Picard. "Come in."

Bissonette stepped through the doorway into the gloomy apartment. Picard understood the message before it was spoken. That Bissonette should call on him was proof that his stature at the Prefecture had taken a serious drop—Bissonette, swaying where he stood, kept on the force only because of his long years of service, reduced now to being the Prefect's errand boy, and unimportant errands at that, for it was well known he would stop at every bistro along the way.

"Having a little target practice?" Bissonette nodded toward the Colt, which Picard still held in his hand.

"I was about to shoot myself."

"Forgive me for interrupting. I can come back later, after you've finished."

Picard walked to the kitchen cupboard, returned with a bottle of cognac and a glass. Bissonette removed his hat, looking at the bottle with a misty glaze across his eyes. His suit was wrinkled, his nose swollen, and he smiled cheerfully as he watched Picard pour the drink.

"You don't look well, Picard," he said, lifting the glass. "Here's to your health." He drained the glass in one gulp. "Yes, I'll have another."

"The Prefect sent you?"

"The Prefect sent me, of course." Bissonette poured the second drink and drained it more slowly. "Do you mind if I smoke my pipe? I'm trying to develop new and better habits." He fumbled in his pocket, came out with matches, studied them for a moment, continued his search for the pipe.

"What message does the Prefect have for me?"

"He wishes you the best, my friend, all the best in the world." The pipe was stuffed clumsily, Bissonette sprinkling tobacco over the table, his suit, and the floor. "He understands you were badly smoked. We all understand, and naturally we're completely sympathetic."

"I'm grateful for your concern," said Picard. "Is there anything else the Prefect wishes me to know?"

"He's eager for you to return to service. Sent me here expressly to tell you . . . of his eagerness . . ." Bissonette's eyes cleared for a moment as he stared across the table at Picard, and Picard saw the truth there, hidden behind the drunkard's clumsiness.

"Out with it," said Picard. "Am I washed up?"

"The general feeling around headquarters . . ." Bissonette's eyes fogged again, stupidity clouding his gaze, but something drove the cloud away and he looked straight at Picard. ". . . yes, I would say so. It was unfortunate that the building you were in burned to the ground. And those on either side of it." He reached for the bottle again. "It causes embarrassment for the Prefect. Won't you join me? I hate to drink alone. A few drinks, a quiet afternoon . . ."

"I'm dismissed then?"

"No, no, no, my friend, of course not. Our Prefect isn't a barbarian. You'll continue on as usual . . . when you're able, when you're well. I must say you're looking poorly, Picard. You need a drink to bring the color back to you. Sit right where you are, I'll get another glass."

Picard sat where he was, staring at the table. Bissonette rattled around in the kitchen and returned with an empty jar, into which he poured a drink for Picard, handing it to him with a smile. "Nothing to be upset about, nothing at all. It's the younger men in the Prefecture who're always making trouble for us veterans. They're a pushy bunch, you know. But the Prefect understands. He asked me to give you your next assignment, when you're ready, of course, when you're able . . ."

"I'm ready. What is it?"

"Just the sort of case I would like to be on myself, were I to go on cases these days, which I don't, because of my unfortunate affliction. You know, don't you, that I've been seeing double for some time now?"

"I didn't know," said Picard, sipping the cognac.

"Heredity. Double vision runs in the family."

"What is my assignment?"

"It's a lovely assignment, lovely. I have the address written down here . . . somewhere . . ." Bissonette searched in his pocket, withdrawing a slip of paper. "Eighty-seven, rue de Richelieu. There's been a fellow entertaining there in luxurious style. No visible means of support. Lazare. Ric Lazare. Came to Paris from Vienna two months ago."

"The Prefect wishes me to look into these apartments?"

"No hurry, Picard. When you're able. It's not a pressing case."

"I perceive that." Picard drained his cognac slowly, staring at the table. "Is there anything else I should know about this man Lazare?"

"There's a hundred-franc admittance to his salon."

"Is he running a show?"

"I've gathered there's a magical game." Bissonette's pipe erupted, sending a burning ember onto his jacket. "A fortune-telling machine . . ." He casually brushed the ember onto Picard's rug, where it smoldered and burned out. "The hundred-franc entrance fee is supposed to put the guests in the proper mood. And then your fortune is unveiled."

Bissonette smiled, burped, and poured himself another drink.

T H E Prefect opened the dossier. "Lazare claims to be Austrian. His source of income is supposedly from estates he owns in Leopoldstadt. We checked with the Bank of Austria here and found Lazare's account is healthy— apparently he's sold portions of his estate to some of our prominent citizens—Madame Westra, Marshal Legère, Prince Thibeault. Frankly, I don't see why they should want to make such purchases."

"What about this fortune-telling business of his?"

"These days every salon must have a fortune-teller. Ric Lazare has hired a Hindoo who mumbles over a crystal ball. Madame Leyette employs a woman who reads feet. I attach no importance to any of it." The Prefect swiveled his chair toward the window. "We live in strange times, Picard, everybody playing at turning tables and such. The other day at the Place de l'Observatoire I myself witnessed a dog translating passages from the Greeks." The

Prefect swiveled back, opened a newspaper on his desk. "There's something in here . . ." He turned the pages. ". . . something about Lazare."

His eyes went down the page, he stopped to read for a moment, then looked up with a smile. "Last night Countess Essena appeared at a ball as Salome, wearing an 'unmentionable costume.' What do you suppose that might have been?"

"A few feathers, perhaps?"

"A troubling thought." The Prefect continued down the page. "Yes, here we are . . ." He handed the paper to Picard, pointing to an account of the Lazare salon.

Picard went through it quickly. The guests were all of the highest station—Duc de Gramont-Caderousse, the Russian millionaire M. de Kougueleff, Prince Paskevitch, the Countess Duplessia. *But the angel of Paris,* wrote the infatuated reporter, *is Madame Lazare, who appeared wearing a net of gold in her hair, an off-the-shoulder gown of cream-colored satin by Laferrière, with arrangements of silver cord decorating the lower part; accessories —bands of velvet, worn on the wrist, ornamented with flowers.*

"Of course you'll act with the usual discretion," said the Prefect. "I don't want Lazare to know we're watching him. Have you a suitable cover?"

"Fanjoy."

"Fanjoy . . . Fanjoy . . . something to do with—diamonds?"

"Pearls," said Picard. "I shall go as Monsieur Fanjoy, the pearl buyer."

The hallway of the Prefecture seemed endless, filled with strange turnings. He went slowly, leaning on his walking stick, but a touch on his sleeve nearly toppled him; he fought to regain equilibrium, to confront a familiar figure—Veniot, of the old guard, Veniot smiling, his face like a walnut, wrinkled, hard.

"You're back to work," said Veniot. "I knew we'd see you soon."

"It's a trifling case," said Picard. "I'm washed up."

Veniot's expression became at once more natural, as he gave up the little show Picard had been observing all day at the Prefecture, put on by those friends of his who tried to conceal the fact they knew he'd been dumped in the turnip bin. "It's unfortunate," said Veniot. "Very unfortunate."

The dizziness hit Picard again, the familiar corridor tilted on its side, and he felt the blood draining from his face. Veniot saw, lent his arm. "Keep moving . . . you mustn't fall here . . . the Prefect's assistant passes at five for his supper . . ."

Picard pretended a resolute step, marched blindly forward, Veniot close beside him, down the corridor, into the courtyard. They stood together, Picard breathing deeply, slowly, Veniot watching him closely, his hand still beneath Picard's elbow.

"Maybe you should rest longer—at a resort."

Picard brought himself up straight, laid the handle of his cane lightly on Veniot's granite jaw. "And drink Vichy water."

"While undressing the maids."

"I'm better now. The air is what I need. A few more days . . ."

"We'll have lunch tomorrow. Something fiery, to thin the blood."

Picard nodded, moved off slowly, conscious of Veniot's eyes upon him. He struggled to keep a straight line, made numerous resolutions about his weight, his abstention from lemon tarts. Turning toward the river, he tried to step smartly, establish a military cadence, the rhythm of his best days. There were many strengths to draw upon. The thousand devils rely on a man forgetting his own power, and force him to his knees, forgetful. Walk, Picard, walk and recall the parade ground, the gleam of sabers.

The Church of St. Germain-l'Auxerrois pealed the four o'clock bells. He came to the Seine, crossed the bridge. The water sparkled green, a stream of liquid jade. A barge passed beneath him and then was slowly gone on the water, on and away, into the twilight of the fall afternoon. He walked to St. Michel, stopped at the doorway of the notorious Grotto of Lilacs café. "Closed again, is it?"

"Once again last night," said the gendarme guarding it, "the cancan dancers exceeded the bounds of decency."

"To have been there."

"I myself was present," said the gendarme, his eyes red and swollen. "There was a conspicuous absence of underwear on the ladies . . ."

"And will it open again tonight?"

"I've been told arrangements are being made about underwear."

Picard walked on, through the winding streets of the Quarter. On the rue de Savoie he was drawn to a window he'd passed many times before. Now he was attracted by the paper stars and moons and by the legend:

Julsca—Fortune

He stepped closer, until his face was reflected in the glass, his top hat crowned by the crescent moon. Tonight I'm going to be Monsieur Fanjoy, virtuoso in pearls. Perhaps Monsieur Fanjoy is interested in his spiritual fortune as well. Indeed, that is why he's making a visit to the salon of Ric Lazare, because he's fascinated by fortune-tellers.

A barefooted little girl greeted him at the doorway, took his hand, and led him without a word into a heavily curtained parlor, where no sun came and a middle-aged gypsy woman sat reading a newspaper.

"Good afternoon," said Picard.

She laid down the newspaper and turned sleepy eyes upon him, then gestured toward a small table, where two chairs faced each other. She was heavy and coarse-featured and joined him at the table with a deck of dog-eared cards.

"Shuffle," she said, handing him the deck.

He fancied himself a shark with cards, had been in great games on the desert, beneath canvas, for big sums of money, for homes that had been left behind, for family heirlooms. for anything a soldier might bring forward as a stake. For one hour on the sand, with an attack expected at any moment, he'd owned a major's villa, six carriages, and a dozen horses, and lost them again on the turn of a card as bullets disintegrated the gambling tent. He shuffled now, mixing the dog-eared cards with lightning speed, but the gypsy woman was not impressed. She had lowered her head and her eyes were closed. He laid the shuffled deck before her, where it remained a moment, until she reached for it, put it to her forehead.

"What is your name?"

He hesitated.

"You have a name," she said, rubbing her forehead with the edge of the deck.

"Paul Fanjoy."

She laid four cards out, face up. "This is your first name," she said, then laid out another row beneath it, again of four, then a third row of six. "This is your last name: F–A–N–J–O–Y. Is that right?"

"Yes."

She studied the cards for a moment, then pointed to the Three of Coins. "You are a craftsman, skilled in your trade."

"That is so," said Picard, smiling.

"And you're troubled by feelings of mediocrity."

The smile left his face as quickly as if she had slapped it. She passed her fingers to the next card in the first row. On the bottom of the card was written:

The Fool

"This is your present situation. You are playing the part of the Fool."

The card showed a jester in belled cap and frivolous costume. Thinking of Monsieur Fanjoy, he felt a distinct discomfort.

"With the Fool is the Queen of Batons. You are a man of common sense, beneath your foolish costume."

Picard looked into the eyes of the woman. She seemed half asleep, but her words struck with amazing clarity. And yet of course it is the atmosphere of the room, and my own mind, which makes the mood and the associations. It's good I came here. I'll be better prepared for Ric Lazare. He won't catch me off guard. I'm already initiated into the mystery of myself!

"Here is your recent past—the Two of Batons. It's upside down, indicating sadness. I see you forcibly restrained by someone, an enemy perhaps?"

"Perhaps," said Picard, feeling the still-red scar on his temple, where Baron Mantes had so forcibly landed the head of a cane. Restrained, indeed.

"Your influence on others," said the woman, pointing to the Valet of Coins. "You're a man of deep concentration, and this is felt by all who come within your field. Nonetheless, you have a tendency to overlook obvious facts."

"Such as?"

"That I cannot say, but beside the Valet is the Cavalier of Coins, indicating limitation because of narrow views. Does that suggest something to you?"

"I'm an enlightened man," said Picard with a smile. "Or at least I think I am."

"You will be going into another country soon—it's here, in the Four of Swords."

"It's usual to see some sort of trip, isn't it?"

The woman looked at him coldly, then pointed to the next card. "Beware of the Hanged Man. You must undergo a change of attitude, a serious transformation, if you are to win."

"Win?"

"You're going to encounter black magic, here, beneath the Hanged Man." She pointed to a card that showed a handsome young man, standing before a table of strange objects, and holding a wand in his hand. "This is the card of the Magician, in the sphere of broad influences. You are going to be deeply moved by magic."

Picard saw the gypsy child standing in the doorway, winked at her. She smiled and ducked away.

"Here is the Sun, your card of accomplishment, which indicates that you may triumph, after some delay." She pointed to the adjacent card. "You are a lawyer?"

The card was Judgment. "No," said Picard, "but . . ." He smiled. ". . . I have something to do with the law."

"You must be careful, then, for it is linked to this card, the Five of Cups, indicating imperfection, a slight flaw."

"How so?"

"I believe it is connected to the Valet of Coins—your tendency to overlook obvious facts."

"Well, how is it all going to turn out?"

"There are the Lovers—here is their card. It is with them you will ultimately be concerned. Are you in love?"

"Hardly."

"The Lovers are sometimes called the Brothers—and one of them always kills the other." She moved her finger to the last card. "This is the High Priestess. It's the card of enlightenment. Perhaps . . ." The woman smiled for the first time, and her sleepy eyes suddenly sparkled. ". . . perhaps you will become an enlightened man, as you say."

"So I can look for a favorable ending?" smiled Picard, laying a large franc note on the table.

"Beware of the Magician, my friend. His card is shining strongly against you."

"I have a few cards of my own," said Picard, and with a bow he left the room, and the building, plunging back into the crisp autumn air. The wind whirled the leaves on the street in a bright dancing ring. The magic ring.

Grandmother called it that . . . when leaves are caught in the wind . . .

He walked into the ring, driving his foot through the little dancing pocket of leaves, scattering them.

T H E grey day surrendered into the arms of night. The lamps of the Quarter were being lit. He began dressing. His evening suit was well made; the leather pistol pouch sewn inside the jacket did nothing to spoil the clean line. From a tobacco tin on his bureau, he scooped out three loose pearls, as well as a pearl stick pin and a pearl ring. They were first quality, purchased by the Prefecture at a significant discount during the liquidation sale of Horace the Rat, as the fence was known, just before the Prefect closed him out of business for good, after which it was understood he would leave the country, which he did, floating head down into the Channel, his complete liquidation brought about, it was believed, by his creditors.

Picard removed one more item from the tobacco tin, a small packet of embossed calling cards, written in the name of Monsieur Paul Fanjoy, Africa Oyster Bed Company.

"Monsieur Fanjoy," said Picard, bowing toward the mirror, "we meet again."

He completed his ensemble with top hat, evening cape, and a slender malacca cane. Monsieur Fanjoy, wealthy boulevardier, ready for a night of prowling. He raised his cane and brought it down in a swift parry-and-thrust, breaking the arm of an imaginary Baron Mantes. The room went spinning and he had to lean on the cane to keep from falling. He breathed deeply and fought for balance. Take it slowly, gently. In any case, Monsieur Fanjoy knows nothing of fighting. He taps his cane daintily as he goes.

He put on thin yellow gloves, shut the door behind him, descended the rickety stairs. In the hallway of the ground floor, he passed the open door of the concierge's room; it was dimly lit and he heard the usual voices of the card-players, a gang of thugs and loafers from the neighborhood. He preferred dark ramshackle buildings like this one, where you could come and go as you please without some damned old woman perched on the landing, demanding your key each time you went out. The bitches ran Paris and he hated them and their old maid's regulations about what you could and could not do in your rooms, whom you could entertain there and who was forbidden to enter. His present concierge would not care if he imported a thousand naked dancing girls and rode with them on elephants up the stairs. The mood of the building was casual; the gentlemen practiced knife-throwing in the halls.

He entered the rue de Nesle and walked the few paces to the rue de Nevers, a perfect little alley in which to tap a man on the skull. As often as he'd walked it, he could not get his body to completely relax there, for the

lane was too tight, too threatening, and he used it now to
tighten his guts. The little lane did its work, its shadows
and stone walls honing his nerves toward readiness.

He exited the narrow alley, onto the quay, tasting the
river air. The worst a man can do is lie in his bed like a
turnip in a bin, rooting slowly in the darkness. Movement, Picard, and the lights of the city, that's what you
need to bring you round; wine and a kick in the belly.
Those who sit at home in their stuffed chair will start
growing stalks out of their head.

He walked onto the bridge, crossed to the Right Bank,
into the massive public courtyards. The lights of the
palace blazed. Seven o'clock, our Emperor is dining with
his beautiful Eugénie. Later he'll slip off to find a whore
somewhere. Long live the Emperor. Rescued last month
in a pimp's alleyway. Wearing a disguise, in search of
love, and nearly assassinated. The Emperor has the spirit
of youth. Refuses to be encrusted by his crown. A wise
man. And here is the rue de Richelieu. This Monsieur
Lazare—right up the street from the palace. Paying
through the teeth for such an address. Fleecing somebody,
I can feel it in my bones. A fortune-telling machine. Grotesque. Our enlightened Empire.

And which of these luxurious houses—but of course,
that one. Bengal lights and colored lanterns. Lit up like
a palace.

Faint sounds from the salon reached him, soft music, the
tinkle of glasses. He entered the glittering courtyard,
crossed to the staircase of the townhouse, where a footman admitted him, taking his card, his cape and hat, and
extending a silver salver. "One hundred francs, Monsieur
Fanjoy, please."

The footman led him up a long hallway and gestured him into the grand parlor. The room was supported by Grecian pillars and hung with heavy gold drapes. Vines were twined around the pillars, and plants of all kinds grew between them, making the entire room a garden. The women were spectacular.

He glanced quickly over the faces, whose outlines were continually being traced in the newspapers. He looked for the cracks in their façade, could tell which ones would be easy game for a blackmailer. Little secrets have a way of playing at the tips of our fingers and in our eyes. The skilled blackmailer sees it and he draws on it, until the secret is his.

At the buffet table he avoided the cream tarts, selected a sandwich of black-jeweled caviar. The essence of the sea burst onto his tongue, strong and mysteriously fishy, precisely the atmosphere of this room, reflected the Inspector, gazing about him.

The gentlemen's vests sparkled with war and service medals. Their faces were proud, distinguished—Lecour the boxing master, what is he doing here? Even he is subdued, Lecour who hits like a mule's kick, acting as if the darkest secret of his life were known.

Picard's eyes were drawn to the far end of the buffet table, to a slender young man who had produced a sheaf of papers from his pocket and was explaining their contents to a second man, of soft sagging face and a freckled dome crowned by a few strands of red hair.

". . . the mine is located here, beyond Banana Point. Our expedition will be outfitted at a native village, approximately three miles from . . ."

Duval the certificate peddler, observed Picard. The

Prefect arrested him last year, outfitting balloon expeditions from a room on the rue du Dragon. Princesse de la Tour d'Auvergne gave him two hundred thousand francs for a lot of hot air. If he has found his way to this salon, it's because he senses some kind of game is afloat. Looking for a piece of it himself.

And there's the fox.

Picard moved nearer to the darkly tanned figure posturing himself against one of the Grecian pillars. The man's slow and languid gestures had apparently hypnotized the young woman who stood with him, for she stared in fascination as he spoke to her, and seemed to sway gently, among the plants and vines that surrounded her swarthy host. A Moroccan bandit, reflected the Inspector, if you saw him strolling through Pigalle . . .

But here, with the gold drapes, the attendant butlers, the velvet suit he wears—transformation. A man of mystery, whose eyes look deep into our souls, into our secrets. And if he looks too deeply, if he perchance perceives a little indiscretion in our private life, why for just a small sum of money he'll keep your secret to himself.

". . . I would say, Countess Lydiatt, that your body is becoming more sensitive to astral influences . . . you have begun to sense them in the air about you . . ."

"But it's true, Monsieur Lazare, every word! I've felt that way for the whole season . . ." The girl blushed, lowering her eyes momentarily, and the fox smiled indifferently, as if Countess Lydiatt's most intimate feelings were of only passing interest to him. But then he brought his jeweled fingers to his chin, supporting his head with a sudden thoughtfulness, as his strangely dazzling eyes grew brighter. "You were visited by an important dream, very recently, something of great urgency . . ."

The girl's eyes opened wide, matching the fox's, and Picard turned away in disgust, toward the buffet table once more. Tell him your dreams, Countess. Pour your whole story into his lap.

Picard was served another cracker of caviar. The red-headed man at the end of the table was still nodding enthusiastically over Duval's bogus portfolio. "Yes, it sounds good. A good investment. I like the ring of it, a touch of adventure, eh?" The man smiled. Picard tried to see the cover of Duval's portfolio, saw only the word

Eldorado

"Shall we meet for lunch tomorrow?" Duval took off his glasses, rubbed them with a silk handkerchief, his eyes clear and innocent as a lamb's. "At my club . . ."

"The Industrialist's, is it?"

"Yes, will two o'clock be convenient?"

"That's fine," said the red-headed man. "And then later perhaps you could come to our place for supper? Suzette was asking for you. She'd especially like to see you again, and hear more about the mine. She's fascinated by Africa, you know."

Picard came directly beside the two men, pretending to be absorbed in the selection of a morsel of cheese. Duval has hooked the fellow completely. But if I have anything to say about it, monsieur, your money will not go out the window, and Duval here will go into a cell once more. "Excuse me," said Picard. "I could not help overhearing you gentlemen." He nodded to the investment portfolio. "You were discussing a gold mine?" He put his hand into his jacket, producing his card. "Paul Fanjoy, Africa Oyster Bed."

Duval studied the card for a moment, then looked up with a smile at the large bluish-white orb which adorned Picard's tie pin. "Pearls, Monsieur Fanjoy?"

"My main business is in the coastal waters," said Picard. "But I'm always looking for another African investment. I know there's gold on the mainland, and plenty of it."

"Paul Fanjoy," said Duval, looking at the card again. "I cannot place the name, Monsieur Fanjoy, but your face is familiar."

"Your club is the Industrialist's? I've been there."

"And you shall be there tomorrow," said Duval. "You'll join Monsieur Bonnat and me for lunch, and we can discuss the mine in greater detail." Duval handed the portfolio to Picard. "Perhaps you know the region . . ."

Picard studied the map, traveling along a spidery blue thread of water through the jungle's green face, deep into the rain forest, to Duval's Eldorado.

"And when does the expedition begin?" He looked up from the map, only to find the eyes of both men cast beyond him, onto a woman in cherry red, her gown exposing the greater part of shoulders and bust, around which she'd arranged some transparent pink tarlatan, a delightfully unsuccessful conceit.

"I haven't seen that much breast since I was weaned," remarked Bonnat.

"And she is . . . ?" Picard reached for a cream tart.

"Madame Lazare, of course," said Duval.

Picard followed her with his eyes as she circulated among her guests. Her naked arms were something you could squeeze a bit, the sort he liked, and he imagined her thighs must be the same, exquisitely plump to cushion a man's fall.

She stopped in the center of the room, chatting with a grey-haired officer, her bosom trembling as she laughed, as she touched her hand to the chain of velvet flowers in her hair, and Picard felt velvet petals opening in his stomach as she glanced toward him. The sensation was unbearably delicious, and he turned away. There was no point in torturing himself.

As if in response to his move, as if she had more interest in those whose eyes were cast away from her, she made toward them, or so Duval reported, under his breath, as Picard reached for another cream tart and replaced it, uneaten. He could feel her approaching, turned slowly, into her dark eyes.

"We are overwhelmed, madame," said Duval, bowing to the hand she extended to him, receiving it in his own and kissing it lightly, upon her dark red gloves.

"I'm so happy you could come. Did your fortune of yesterday ring true?"

"Completely."

Madame Lazare smiled. "Ric is rarely wrong."

"How does he do it, madame?" asked Picard.

"My husband is a rare being," said Madame Lazare, slowly opening a silken fan across her lips. Again Picard felt a maddening sensation pass through his body, as if the woman had reached an invisible hand into his stomach and was toying with him there, upon the very nerve of bliss. Her eyes lingered with his for a moment, vaguely curious, before she turned to Bonnat.

"And how is your wife, monsieur?"

"Fine, yes, very fine. I must bring her here again. She enjoyed it immensely. But she won't tell me what your husband's machine said to her."

"There are secrets," said Madame Lazare, bending forward to take a tiny sandwich from the buffet table. The three men leaned as she did so, like drunkards teetering on the edge of an abyss. She straightened again, still smiling, as if she had not just revealed her own secrets. Picard wanted to rip the pearl ring off his finger and hand it to her on his knees.

He was spared by the arrival of the butler, who came up to them and bowed to Bonnat, holding out at the same time a small golden tray with Bonnat's card on it.

"Here I go again," said Bonnat with a laugh, taking his card and following the butler across the room, toward a large oak door leading out of the parlor.

"And you, monsieur—" Madame Lazare turned to Picard. "What brings you to our salon?"

"These," said Picard, reaching into his pocket and bringing out a midnight-blue handkerchief, which he slowly opened, revealing three large glowing pearls. Madame Lazare held out her hand and Picard put the pearl-laden handkerchief into it. "I'm hoping your husband will tell me where to find more such beauties."

"My husband is a collector too. Perhaps he can help you." Her gown was against his leg, her perfume in his brain, and her fingers touched his lightly as she handed back the handkerchief.

The sound of a slammed door made them turn. Bonnat came toward them, his face as red as his hair, his lips set in a hard scowl. Raising his hand, he laid the back of it across Duval's cheek with a loud crack.

Duval stood silent for a moment, then spoke in a quiet voice. "Very well."

"Tomorrow at dawn," said Bonnat. "At the southeast gate of the Montparnasse cemetery."

"A suitable location," said Duval. "Pistols for two and coffee for one."

Bonnat started to say more, then turned and walked away, out of the parlor, his footsteps echoing in the silence that had fallen over the salon. Duval picked up the crumpled piece of paper Bonnat had hurled at his feet.

"What is it?" asked Madame Lazare.

Duval glanced at the paper and then folded it, putting it in his pocket. "As you say, madame, there are secrets."

"His wife?" she asked softly.

"You are too perceptive." Duval smiled, Bonnat's handprint slowly disappearing from his cheek.

"What are you going to do?" asked Picard, feeling that he must stop the duel.

"Do? There is only one thing a man of honor can do. I'm leaving Paris at once."

"I'm happy there will be no bloodshed," said Madame Lazare. "It doesn't do to carry such things to extremes." She smiled, a flickering scorn in her eyes, for both of them. She extended her hand to Picard, and turned away. He studied her movements as she crossed the room—beneath the elegance of the hostess there was something else, a hint of the gypsy dancer, of wine and taverns, her hips looking as if they wanted to roll when she walked. But it was all hidden, or nearly so, this dark abandon, veiled by the propriety and wealth of the rue de Richelieu.

Duval flourished the Eldorado portfolio again, tapping the gold embossment with his finger. "Has Bonnat spoiled your taste for adventure, Fanjoy? Or do you still love a mine?"

"What happens in people's bedrooms is all the same to me."

"Good, good, then you and I shall meet as planned, tomorrow at my club." Duval lowered his voice conspiratorially. "But how do you suppose this fellow Lazare gets his information?"

"A network of informers," said Picard, regretting at once that he'd spoken a policeman's sentence, but Duval paid no attention, was already moving toward Lazare. Picard crossed the room beside him. Lazare had seated himself, with a number of young ladies nearby him. The ladies looked at Duval curiously, for by now they had divined, without the use of a fortune-telling machine, what the slap in his face had meant.

"Your oracle is a most efficient spy," said Duval, speaking from behind Lazare's chair.

Lazare looked up, turning his head slightly over his shoulder toward Duval. "It is only a toy, monsieur."

His wife had reached alongside him, to an ornate music stand, from which she'd taken a stringed instrument of obvious antiquity. "Play for us, Ric," she said, handing him the instrument. Its wood was black, highly polished and shaped in the form of a snake, with four strings running from tail to lip.

Lazare's long fingers touched the strings, and the serpent's fourfold tongue twanged softly, exotically, a tune like no other Picard had heard. The ancient instrument responded with delicate reverberation, the snake's puffed hollow body echoing the minor air, as a spell fell over the parlor.

There was something in the song—Picard could not remain aloof from it. A strange feeling came over him, the feeling that he was rootless, homeless, an endless wanderer. For an instant his Paris was gone, and the jeweled women were stars, twinkling in a vast empty space.

The bass string returned, thumping softly, as if to an incessant drumbeat, and Picard felt still more alone, on the distant wind. Blown upon a carpet, floating out upon the finely woven song, he felt himself returning to Algeria, to the war. The salon of dreams was far behind him and he was racing on the sands toward the lamplight of a tent. He had it all in his hands—youth, the reins of a good horse, the music of a military encampment calling him.

Lazare's jeweled fingers flashed, ending the song abruptly, dramatically, the last bass note dying softly as the room was held in suspension, Picard no less than the others, as the dream dissolved, a dream one should certainly not forget.

He found himself staring down at the magnificent carpet which covered the salon floor—a Persian rug woven in patterns that suggested ever-deepening webs and wells. And the hanging vines around us, how easily one escapes. Magic carpets to the stars, noble suckers, magic carpets for all!

A young bearded man went toward Lazare; the fellow's clothes were ordinary, his manner that of an observer, a fact which Picard affirmed a moment later when the young man identified himself as a journalist and took a pad and pen from his pocket. "Did you write that piece yourself, Monsieur Lazare?"

"It was given to me by a friend," said Lazare.

"And whom might that be?"

"The vulture-priestess of El Kab."

"El Kab? That's an Egyptian city, is it not?"

"It had another name, when the priestess played for me."

"And when were you traveling in Egypt, Monsieur Lazare? Recently?"

"In the forty-third century B.C."

"The forty-third century?"

"Our king was known as the Scorpion," said Lazare, placing the ancient instrument down. "I believe it was actually he who composed the song, though I received it from his attendant priestess."

"A moment, Monsieur Lazare, a moment please! Are you saying you learned this song five thousand years ago?"

An elegant young woman, adorned with a massive chignon held by a startling diamond pin, came forward, her body obviously still charmed by the music. "I have heard you tell others differently about this song, Monsieur Lazare."

"Have I?" The host smiled. "Oh well, it has undergone many transformations . . ."

"You said the other night it was written by the father of Cleopatra."

"The song, dear child, is a traveler through time. It visits now one fellow, and now another . . ."

Lazare's voice grew softer then, and the young woman moved closer to him, as the reporter came away from the little tête-à-tête shaking his head, and joining Duval and Picard at the wine table.

"He would have us believe he was alive five thousand years ago," muttered the reporter, accepting a snifter of brandy.

"And do you?" asked Duval.

"I . . . I don't know."

"It strikes me, monsieur, that you might be interested in the opening of a new gold mine, in Africa . . ."

"Monsieur Fanjoy?"

Picard turned. The butler was standing beside him, and the gold tray was extended. On it was the card of Paul Fanjoy, Africa Oyster Bed Company, and across the bottom of the card was written:

25 seconds, no more!

Picard walked in the tiptoeing way of his foppish puppet, Monsieur Fanjoy. He was conscious of the eyes of others upon him, for now he was the chosen guest, about to be initiated into the mysteries. He smiled insipidly, acting altogether naïve and playful as he followed the butler across the room, toward the large oak door.

They walked through the doorway, into a hall lit by arabesque lamps. Ahead of them was another door, carved with floral designs, and it opened from within as Picard approached.

A tall Hindoo in white robe and turban awaited him inside. The room was windowless. Small candles burned in twisted-silver holders. The Hindoo led Picard to a snake-legged table, on which a crystal ball was set. Picard looked into the ball, saw nothing in its spherical depths.

But the incensed atmosphere and the flickering candles produced a momentary illusion—the room seemed to curve gently around him, as if he were standing inside a transparent bubble. Lazare's operation is all suggestiveness—strange backdrops and dim lights, effects to weaken the mind and make the imagination run riot. I'll wager people see all sorts of things in that ball.

The Hindoo took Picard by the elbow and moved him to another table, on which a small telegraph machine was mounted. The machine started to click; the Hindoo opened a drawer in the table, beneath the telegraph instrument, and withdrew a piece of paper which he thrust into Picard's hand. A tiny chime sounded somewhere in the room, and the butler entered.

"This way, Monsieur Fanjoy," he said, leading his guest back into the dimly lit corridor.

"One moment," said Picard, stopping beneath a lamp. He opened the piece of paper.

PAUL PICARD—THE SPY WILL DIE

The butler opened the door to the parlor and Picard stepped through. The puppet, Monsieur Fanjoy, was completely gone, relegated to the everlasting scrap heap of punctured disguises. Picard tried to get his bearings, felt ridiculous, a laughing-stock.

He saw the host, then, leaning against a window in the corner of the room, withdrawn from the guests. Picard went toward him, the swift poison of anger spreading through his veins. He wanted to break a few things apart, among them, Lazare's neck. He suppressed his violence; the monster raged inside him instead, smashing the chandeliers and coffee table in his liver and stomach, ruining his digestion, but it's considerably better than ruining number 87, rue de Richelieu, thought Picard, as he closed the gap between himself and his host. The Prefect would not take kindly to such a brawl. Go calmly, Picard, you're not in the army any more.

"Monsieur Lazare?"

"Yes?"

"You have threatened me with this note."

"But of course." Lazare was quietly confident. Picard observed Duval moving closer, eavesdropping on the conversation. The host smiled at Picard and gestured toward the wine table. "Drink with me, Inspector, and forget you were ever given this assignment. It will be much the wiser move for you to make."

Picard's monster flung an upholstered chair through his gall bladder; he turned, walked through the crowded salon toward the door, the bit of telegraph paper still crumpled in his fist. The polished floor of the hallway reflected the round yellow wall lamps, and each step he took was into a faintly glowing sphere.

The footman awaited him at the outer door, producing his cape and hat from the cloakroom. He slipped into them, couldn't shake the notion that Lazare was somehow following him, his countenance concealed in the glow of the yellow wall lamps, his shadow gliding unseen in the muted depths of the glistening parquet floor. But the hall was empty, save for Duval, who received his own cape from the footman and stepped with Picard into the courtyard.

"Inspector? Did I hear him address you as a police inspector?"

"Yes," snarled Picard. "So watch your step, Duval."

"No one's to be trusted these days," sighed Duval, as they walked through the iron gate to the rue de Richelieu. Duval hailed a carriage, climbed into it, and opened the window. "Can I leave you someplace? No? Then good hunting, Inspector. And remember, Eldorado Investments welcomes all investors, no matter how small." The driver cracked his whip and the carriage rolled away.

PICARD walked slowly away from the Lazare house-hold, into the lights and traffic of the boulevard Montmartre. How did Lazare know I was coming? One of his spies at police headquarters, perhaps. A logical place for one. It's happened before, headquarters troubled by a leak, subsequently plugged by hot lead. I smell fried potatoes.

He found the seller, an old woman with a portable stove. She handed him a portion of the potatoes, wrapped in white paper, and he walked on, toward Pigalle.

Lazare knows how to unnerve his guests, I'm still feeling strange. But in truth, Picard, you've felt strange for half your life. Too much cognac, too many all-night card games, depravity in general, and most recent, your two-story fall from a burning building. These things do not lead to inner steadiness.

I feel another of my worthless resolutions coming on.

He finished his potatoes, threw the paper away, un-satisfied, knowing it was the type of case that would cause inordinate hunger for weeks, months, for as long as it took to nail Lazare.

He paused before a crêpe seller's stand, thought better of it, moved on toward the Café Orient. If one sampled too much street food an unpleasant rash could develop. His face had swollen like an overripe tomato while fol-lowing Cajetan Seveck, the white slaver.

He was like you, Monsieur Lazare, with great dreams of conquest. Wanted to rule the Empire. You can compare notes with him, over a tin plate in the penitentiary.

The glass doors of the Café Orient had yellow dragons painted on them, yellow with hollow eyes, illuminated by lights from within the café. *Here is Lazare's secret*, whispered the dragons as he pushed through the swinging glass, moving its dragons aside.

He took a table on its glass-enclosed terrace, glanced around at the array of thieves, smugglers, and pimps who sat in the flickering candlelight. He hoped that someone in the café of bad company would prove annoying, so that he might knock a few heads together—and so he was left alone, steeping in the atmosphere of tobacco, sauer-kraut, and stolen goods. The brazier glowed, casting a dancing light on the terrace, where the voices remained low, and the dancing light made the underworld faces still more menacing, like denizens of fire. He thought of others he'd known from this quarter, St. Gervais, the bodyguard of David Orléans, who could break a six-inch board with his head, Abdul the Bird, ruler of the rooftops of Paris. These, and others, haunted the grillwork of the brazier, played amongst the coals. He'd gone against them and they were dead, reduced to phantom memories, to ashes.

And now Lazare. But how to take him—no good sniffing around his salon, he's in complete control there. Speak with his guests, perhaps, those with whom he's had financial dealings. But if he's blackmailing them, they aren't going to speak out.

Face it, Picard, you want to take a jaunt to Vienna, see some sights, recuperate a bit in the country, expenses paid by the Prefecture, and pick up Lazare's threads along the way. Much better than talking to a bunch of idiots so dumb they've let him swindle them. Speak to the Viennese police, pin the bastard down the sure way, right through his velvet wings.

He sat back in his chair, drumming his fingers in anticipation of the journey. A young woman, alone at the end of night, saw his restlessness and moved in. She was a brunette in mauve, her eyelids painted with some dark witchery, and she slipped into the seat beside him, already smiling, for she knew she'd hooked him perfectly.

He nodded slowly. The firelight played upon her face, her coiled chignon; I'll take it down, remove the pins and see it spread upon her pillow.

He reached out, touched the tiny bell earrings which descended from the smooth swaths of her hair.

"Do you wish something?" she asked, at the ringing of the bells.

"I do."

She smiled again, and looked down at her shiny black boots, one dangling above the other, her legs crossed and revealing only the slightest bit of pale-blue stocking.

"Shall we go then?" said Picard, standing. She stood

with him, and slipped her arm into his as they left the café. Her black satin jacket became one with the dark street for a moment, until they stepped beneath the lamppost, and she was radiant again, her jacket sewn with a pale thread that caught the light, revealing a faint diamond-shaped pattern—which suddenly became the hundred gleaming eyes of a Hindoo sorcerer.

"Are you unwell?" she asked, for he'd paused in the street, a feeling of suffocation upon him.

"It's nothing," he said. "I had some wine . . ."

"The wine of the Café Orient isn't fit to wash one's feet in."

They walked along Pigalle, and she stopped at a tenement not unlike his own, where no questions were asked, and where the stairs were similarly teetering and filthy. She carefully raised the hem of her gown, above the garbage and broken bottles on the second landing. Perhaps sensing his thoughts, she turned and smiled. "It's a ruin, I know."

"But you . . ." he said, gesturing to her beauty.

"I too am ruined," she said with a laugh, taking a key from her beaded purse.

She opened the door, and the room was the usual sort of Pigalle hole, an indelible smell of old wine and stale tobacco permeating it, the walls cracked and peeling. Generations of drifters had used it, and Picard felt at home, though not completely, for there was a delicate feminine thing which sought to hold its own against the smell, the dreariness. Her table had a lace cloth, her windows were hung with soft curtains, and her open closet was a silken tabernacle, where brocaded flowers bloomed in shadow and lovely butterflies danced. She had just now removed her boots, and was seated on the bed, wiggling her toes within her stockings.

Picard, still in his cape, knelt at her feet, held them gently in his hands. She leaned back, stretched her legs out; her stockings were embroidered with a design of dark-blue clocks. The voluminousness of her underwear made further exploration difficult; their fingers went together to the buttons which held her gown. It came off easily, leaving her arms and shoulders bare. The floorboards rumbled, the windows rattled.

"They're working nights," she said, dropping the strap of her camisole. "Blasting in the sewers."

"No," he said, helping her lower the other strap. "It's because of you the room shakes."

She smiled; a single candle burned in a stone lantern beside the bed, and the flame was fanned by passing petticoats, gently tossed toward a chair. He saw that the clocks upon her stockings continued upward till they were met by red lace garters; when the garters came away her soft white flesh was imprinted with momentary rings that faded even before he placed his lips upon the peach fuzz of her thighs.

"Your jacket," she whispered, opening the buttons; her fingers touched the smooth butt of his revolver and stiffened, but he removed his jacket with an innocent smile, hanging it over the bedpost.

Her perfume reigned now, obliterating the wine and tobacco smell of the room. Naked she was even more lovely, and she knelt on the bed, waiting as Picard stepped out of his underwear. "I think you might crush me," she said, seeing his barrel-framed body.

Picard stretched out beside her on the bed, taking the

pins from her hair. It tumbled around her shoulders; her eyes were still amused by his physique, which she took in slowly, running her fingers over his shoulders, his neck, twining her fingertips in the tangle of grey-black hair that covered his rock-hard chest. His gut was where his torso weakened, where all the lemon tarts had settled, and she rolled the fat playfully, lingering on the scar that crossed his belly like an obscene grin. "Someone carved you badly, darling."

"There was a large stone in my bladder," said Picard. "The largest ever seen in French medicine. Large and perfectly formed."

She knelt between his legs and brought her lips to the scar, kissing it gently. "Your surgeon was a butcher."

"He was an American dentist." Picard reached toward the chair on which his jacket was slung and put his hand into the vest pocket. "I carry the stone with me wherever I go."

She raised her head, looked at him curiously.

"Here," he said, taking the largest of the three brilliant pearls from his handkerchief. "You may have it."

She laughed and took the pearl in her hand. "A perfect fake."

"Have it appraised before you throw it away."

Her eyes narrowed. "It's real?"

Picard reached into his jacket again. "My card."

"Africa Oyster Bed Company." The young woman looked up with a grin. "Are you good bed company, Monsieur Fanjoy?"

"We'll see," said Picard, drawing her to him, and turning her, so that her back was to him. They lay that way, stretched out against each other, and he slipped his left arm beneath her ribs and wrapped his right arm around her waist, so that he could squeeze both her breasts.

"Especially the left one, Monsieur Fanjoy," she said softly; he gave it careful attention, laying his palm against the nipple and rubbing it quickly and lightly. The sewer crew blasted again, rattling the street, the foundations, her few dishes.

"Is it me, Fanjoy?" she asked, putting her hands between her legs and taking hold of him, putting him where she wanted him.

"Yes," he said, kissing her shoulders and stroking her gently. She pressed back against him; it was his favorite position, for he knew he was too heavy for women, and he was also lazy. This way he could lie like a magnificent pig, fondling her breast, fondling her little wet beard. He'd seen a painting somewhere—the Empress riding to Fontainebleau—it came to him now, then faded, and other things came and went, a gondola, the smell of lime-tree flowers. Is it her perfume, the essence of lime-tree flowers?

"With the whole hand, Fanjoy," she said in a gently pleading voice.

He could feel the rhythm of her pleasure and he toyed with it, steering it with his fingers and his slow deep thrusts. He was in control; one learns certain things only after the hair on one's balls has turned grey; he was happy to steer her, concentrating completely on her pleasure. Her breasts were small, the left one extremely sensitive; the blasting powder made the candle flame dance again, and she moved her hips faster, as if the explosions were indeed taking place inside her.

"Stop," he said softly, into her ear, and she stopped

while he caught his breath and cooled a little, but he didn't let her cool; his fingers moved between her legs, slowly, and her wild racing became a dreamlike coiling and un- coiling. He felt her place exactly, knew just how far she had to go, and he took her there as slowly as he could, making her desire double up against itself, crash and magnify itself. As she coiled toward the edge, just as her spring began to snap, he stopped and she hung suspended over the depths.

The Empress came by again, in a boat filled with her handmaidens and a Turkish oarsman. They sailed slowly along, disappearing into the black reaches of his mind, trailing only a few bright bubbles.

"Oh, please, Fanjoy, Fanjoy . . ."

He pressed his face into her hair; it was dry and stiff from acids and curling irons, like the hair of a mare. "Please," she groaned, "please, I can't wait . . ."

He slid his fingers back into her slippery lips, drummed his fingertips, lightly, as he'd been doing when she first saw him, drummed her over the edge. She fell with a long laughing moan, tangled her ankle back around his, trying to drag him with her. He let go, into her laughing chasm, his body dissolving in ecstasy, madness, annihilation, and out of the darkness he heard the voice of Madame Lazare speaking softly in his ear, *There are secrets*, she said, and Duval echoed her voice, *As you say, madame, there are secrets*.

Picard gasped, felt himself in Lazare's clutches, felt lost and disintegrating, a fool with a girl in the night, caught in a trap he cannot see, a trap which closes softly, and then it was over and he felt only the soft, gently closing lips of the young woman, opening and closing on him, draining him sweetly and completely. It's only a screw, one of a thousand, a million, the night, the night. The stairway rattled again, he thought perhaps someone had fallen down it, perhaps I'm falling down it, down it. He reached far into the blackness, discovering lime-tree flowers, candlelight, the young girl's bare shoulders. He was looking at them, she was soaked with sweat, and he was already feeling the morning train to Vienna.

"Stay there . . . just a moment more," she said. He liked her sobbing laugh, knew that he could easily fall for her, and was anxious to clear out before it happened. After a few weeks with this one, I'd be groveling, as usual, or wanting to clip her on the jaw. Better not to suffer that again; don't look in her heart too long.

He felt the flopping in his stomach, where she had gained a hold on him, where he was helpless and already loving her. A helpless pig about love, he understood himself too well.

He found his undershirt. If we're lucky we'll never meet again. He glanced back and saw the look in her eyes. Young girls sometimes fall quickly too. But not for long. In two weeks she'd be using my head for a soup bowl. Clear out, Picard, while you still can. Where are my shorts?

She knelt at the edge of the bed, ran her fingers up his leg, to his groin, fondling him there. "Your jewel, dear Fanjoy," she said, touching his battered, half-hidden nut. "What happened to it?"

"Did you know St. Gervais, the bodyguard of David Orléans? He hung out in this neighborhood."

"Did he . . . ?"

"He kicked me in the jewel."

"Men are so stupid." She helped him close the buttons on his pants. "And you, what did you do to him?"

"He was buried with his rib cage torn out."

"How disgusting . . ."

"But necessary, for he certainly would have torn out mine." He went to the mirror, adjusted his tie. Within the glass he watched her return to bed. She lay down and placed the pearl in her belly button, staring at it, smiling faintly.

"The perfect setting," he said, turning back to her. It was all right now, the danger had passed. He felt his freedom, and hers, and just now they were two swift birds of the night.

"Will it pay my rent?" she asked.

"It will."

"You're a gentleman, Monsieur Fanjoy."

"No," he said, "I'm a fool." He looked away from her again, for they could easily lose their wings, especially if she gave him any sort of compliment. A pig with women, a simple and incurable pig.

"Perhaps I'm the fool," she said, "believing this is real." She toyed with the pearl, setting it between her breasts. "Perhaps you're just a liar . . ."

"Tomorrow, when you find an honest jeweler . . ."

She looked up, smiling. "But even if you're a liar, Fanjoy, I don't care. Come back to bed with me. Give me some more of that." She closed her eyes, and squeezed her thighs together.

He fastened his cape, found his cane and hat. In less than a week with this one. In three days I would be enslaved.

He opened the door, turned toward her as he stepped

into the hall. She was seated on the bed, looking at him,
raising her hair up over her head.

I am already enslaved. Fly, Picard, fly!

He went quickly down the creaking stairs, past the
broken bottles, into the street. What a wonderful girl.
Don't look back for the address—but I know her building,
could pick it out of a million others.

A winged pig of love, flying over the gutter.

He walked slowly through the darkness of the late hour.
Café dancers stood in the shadows of a doorway, smoking,
speaking low, apparitions in the smoke.

He stopped in front of the Hôtel Royal. Its restaurant
was still open, couples seated by candlelight in the windows. And in the dark wreath that surrounded the
building there floated a memory, of Abdul the Bird.

Picard walked beside the fence of the hotel, tapping
his cane lightly on the iron spikes. That one down there,
I marked it with my pocketknife.

He found the spike, with the notch cut in it, and sighted
over it, to the rooftop, into the eyes of a grinning gar-
goyle, who'd been grinning the night he and the Arab
had wrestled on the ledge. His dagger in my ribs up there.
But my bootheel in his face, and over the edge he went,
Abdul the Bird, unable to fly, after all, impaling himself
on this spike.

Picard rubbed the spike for luck. Little superstitions,
yes. Small ceremonies to preserve one's confidence.

He tapped along the rest of the fence, felt his cane pass
through the last spike, as if it were made of smoke, then
saw that in fact there was no spike at all, he'd seen a last
one where there was none—but I know, yes I know
which spike that one is. It's the one Abdul's ghost has

planned for me. He waits with it in the darkness, waits for me to fall.

Walk on, Picard, the river lights are calling.

Lamplight and moon, splashed on the river—he approached slowly, heard voices from the water, on the houseboat docked there, saw the dog, the water wolf who sat by himself on deck, watching the river.

The dog turned, feeling someone's gaze upon him, his eyes the tiniest lights on the river, and the most expressive. He stared at Picard a moment, then turned slowly back toward the river, resuming his watch over the passing darkness, in which humanity played the least interesting part.

From the Quarter came the Spanish songs, the Spaniards drunk now and renewing themselves with melodious memory, of Granada, Málaga. Picard went through the music, humming as he passed them, his barrel tones sombre and few, something like a hound's growling.

His stomach was growling as well; he pushed through the doors of the Restaurant Hindustan.

"Paul!" Armand came toward him, hand outstretched.

"How're you, amigo?"

"I have an incomparable stew tonight."

⁓

"Don't let that bit of mold trouble you, Paul." Armand set down a disreputable little bread basket, whose straw edges bore the marks of a rodent who'd sharpened his teeth there.

"What do you know about Ric Lazare?"

"His wife is a . . . ." Armand made an obscene noise with his mouth.

"Anything about Lazare himself?"

"The usual crap. You know how thieves exaggerate."

Picard took a piece of bread, examined it carefully, set it back down. "Lazare is known to them?"

"He cleaned out Vienna, so they say."

"How did he perform there?"

"Very well, to judge by the joint he's purchased on the rue de Richelieu. That stew is something, eh?"

Picard stared at the grey concoction of grease and bones, regretting he'd consumed as much of it as he had. "Aside from the hairs floating there . . ."

"It's that Turk I have cooking for me," said Armand, grabbing the bowl and looking into it. "I told that son of a bitch to trim his mustache!"

Armand led the way back to the kitchen. The Turk and a grizzled old dishwasher were taking turns with a slingshot, stoning a small plaster statue of Louis Napoleon. Louis's head had been shot off. The Turk was drawing back the rubber, let fly a stone that tore the Emperor's legs off and the little statue tumbled over. In the excitement the Turk dropped his cigar butt in the large soup pot. He stirred around in it for a few moments, but was unable to locate the stub.

"Here, Paul," said Armand, taking the slingshot, "have a shot."

"I've no quarrel with Louis," said Picard, smiling.

Armand placed a stone in the sling. "This, Louis, is from the peerless restaurateur you seek to ruin." He turned to Picard. "You know our sovereign has decreed that this street shall be widened and my café torn down?"

"I didn't know."

"There will be no more incomparable stew . . ." Armand took aim. The band stretched to its ultimate length, the sling snapped, the stone flew to its mark, shattering what was left of the Emperor. The dishwasher made a mark on the kitchen wall, which was already covered by numerous score lines. He turned to Armand and saluted.

"We've destroyed one hundred Louis Napoleons, my captain."

"This calls for a celebration." Armand went to the wine cabinet, brought out a dusty bottle and held it to the light. "A disgusting wine from one of the worst years." He opened the bottle and filled four glasses. Putting the wine to his lips, he tasted it and grimaced. "Distinguished by its superb sourness. How was your stew, Paul? Tell me truthfully."

"Matched only by this wine," said Picard, pouring it into a large rubber plant beside the kitchen door.

"Omar," said Armand, pointing toward the Turk, "is the worst chef in Paris. I am fortunate to have him."

The Turk bowed ceremoniously and Armand put his arm around Picard's shoulder, leading him back to the dining room, through the aisle of empty tables.

"Come by for breakfast, Paul. Omar will be preparing a marvelous omelette. First he throws it on the floor . . ."

"Know anything else about Lazare?"

"He can drink poison," said Armand. "Yes, I'm not kidding you. Some Viennese dumbbell challenged him to a duel and Lazare chose the weapon—a bottle of poison which they shared. The dumbbell died, of course, and Lazare is in Paris, entertaining on the rue de Richelieu. But I'd like to see him drink a glass of this little wine and live to tell of it." Armand spit a mouthful out the door, as Picard stepped into the street.

The Spaniards were still singing. He walked through their ranks, attempted another growl or two. A few minutes' walk brought him to the door of his tenement. The card game continued in the concierge's room. A broken claret glass lay in the doorway, fragments of it scattered around the hall. Last month there'd been a contest among the gentlemen, to see who could kick a bottle, barefooted, furthest up the stairs. A ridiculous affair, which Picard was ashamed to admit he'd won.

He climbed slowly to his apartment, let himself into the gloom, undressed in darkness. The Spaniards had drifted into the narrow rue de Nesle and were leaning up against the dead end of it, singing of the Alhambra in the echoing lane. They led him into sleep with their sad lament, to a street in an unknown land, where the streetlamps were crystal balls, one after another along an endless avenue. He followed it over the horizon and down, walking the great glittering thoroughfare. In each of the crystal lamps he saw figures moving, small and luminous, their bodies forming the radiance of the lamps. With sudden astonishment he found himself coming up and around to the spot from which he'd begun. His avenue was a ring of silver, and the lampposts were jewels which decorated the ring.

Looking up, he saw high above him the giant who wore the jeweled ring upon his finger. Horrified, Picard realized that his own body was no bigger than a flea, crawling along the rim of the giant's ring.

He woke, heard a Spaniard vomiting in the gutter. It was dawn. The night had gone by in an instant.

II

THE VALET OF COINS

"No, Lazare is no citizen of Austria, nor does he own any property in Leopoldstadt." The Viennese Chief of Police opened his desk drawer and removed a brass water pipe, the bowl of which he filled with dark wet tobacco. "There is, however, a superb prison in Leopoldstadt. Perhaps you would care to visit it. I can contact the warden."

"No," said Picard, "I think not."

"The insane asylum, then?" The Chief placed a piece of glowing charcoal in the bowl. "Upon request . . ." He puffed on a silken-wrapped hose. ". . . the patients are exhibited and beaten for special guests. I could arrange . . ."

"Thank you, no," said Picard. "You have nothing on this man Lazare?"

"We know who he is, naturally. He operated here for months." The Chief surrounded himself with a cloud of smoke, the fumes of which made Picard lean forward dizzily. The Chief smiled. "You're admiring the aroma of my tobacco. A mixture of spice and molasses." He pointed to the gurgling brass chamber. "Essence of rose and saffron in the water. It is the style in Kashmir. Have you been there? I have another tube for this infernal thing, you can join me . . ."

"I must refrain . . ."

"Yes, the smoke is rather strong. Comes from a marvelous little shop, you must visit it, the Black Mother of God." The Chief continued puffing and looked up with a sheepish grin. "Strong, very strong. Occasionally it renders me unconscious."

"About Lazare . . ."

"He swindled a fortune out of our nobility. I know this for a fact, but no complaint came forth, nor was a single charge laid against him. Are you certain you wouldn't care to hook on the other tube? Tobacco like this . . ."

"Why weren't charges brought against him?"

"Fear, I should think. I put a man on his track, one of my best men. You'll find this hard to believe, no doubt—" The Chief leaned forward, the silken hose hanging from the corner of his mouth. "He visited Lazare's salon, on Augustin Strasse, a very good address, you know. Lazare had—a crystal ball. His guests looked into it, a parlor game, that sort of thing. My man looked into it and saw . . ." The Chief paused, rekindled his charcoal. ". . . saw himself lying dead on the pavement. He reported back to me, terribly rattled."

"And . . . ?"

"He was found dead on the pavement the next day. On Augustin Strasse."

"The cause of death?"

"Apoplexy." The Chief inhaled slowly, blew a long stream of smoke in the air, his face growing suddenly pale. "If I should collapse . . . would you be good enough to . . . ring for my secretary . . ."

Picard handed a tumbler of water, to the Chief, who sipped it, beads of sweat breaking out on his forehead. He pushed the pipe away, stared at the smoldering bowl. "Well . . . I made a . . . thorough inquiry into Lazare." He slowly wrapped the silken hose into a coil, and sprinkled water in the bowl, sending a sizzling cloud into the air. "I could find no trace of him anywhere else in Europe. He came to us out of the mists. If you want my advice, let him run his course in your city. Let him have his way —if you value your life."

"Surely you don't think he caused the death of your detective?"

"A word to the wise, Inspector. There are very few sidewalks in our city and the traffic is swift, so watch your step. I was nearly run down by a carriage yesterday. Sorry I have nothing more for you on this Lazare fellow. Take care then, adieu . . ."

Picard went through the streets of the city, descending into the dark passageways which had been tunneled beneath the great monolithic buildings, and came out again, a bloodhound with his nose in the wind, chasing a fox who'd left no track.

He entered a lane filled with the carts of peasant tradesmen. They were Greeks and Hungarians and Moldavians, all in native dress. The street was dry and the passing carriages raised the dust; he and Veniot had found the track of Roger Givan, the bomb-throwing anarchist, while staring at an exhibit of artificial teeth. One never knows—the mind is vast, and works with secret precision. Threads, the hidden threads.

That's my card, Monsieur Lazare; you have your fortune-telling machine which tells you all, and I have learned that the earth itself will play when the chase is on. Something will appear, of that I'm certain. Call me superstitious, and think of me as an easy target for your hocus-pocus. But I'm speaking of real magic, Lazare, which no man can control.

He found himself drawn to a narrow canyon-like street, and walked along it, in the shadow of high noble buildings where Austrian princes were entertaining their ladies this winter afternoon. Candles burned in the high windows, and servants came and went, while Picard paused, watching the inner life of the street, his nerves quivering delicately, as they had when he and Veniot were searching for Givan, through this same city. The air had positively crackled, and strange pieces were moved right beneath their noses. Even the phlegmatic Veniot was convinced of it—an invisible hand was at play in the chase.

The street was joined by an intriguing little alleyway which he followed, walking past a row of servants' quarters. An old man in livery was struggling up the alley, a bucket of water in each hand, drawn from a fountain at the alley's end. He entered a kitchen doorway; Picard heard the voices of the kitchen staff for a moment, before they were sealed again behind a heavy wooden door. He continued on toward the fountain; it was a humble, utilitarian creation—for the purpose the old man had put it to —water for the adjoining households. But the Viennese soul could not resist adding a few grotesque pieces of stonework—a bench, and an ancient statue, dragged from somewhere and stuck down, to give visitors to the alleyway something to remember.

Picard was glad of the bench; his head had started to ache, where the Baron had clubbed him. Maybe the Baron's thinking of me. We're beaten down by enemies, by life, and the pain is inevitable, raise the head slowly, slowly . . .

He looked toward the ancient statue, saw now that it was an old tombstone, a block of stone carved in the shape of a heart, with a skull atop it.

His own heart began to beat violently, and a feeling of doom swirled around him. He closed his eyes, trying to relax. His head was ringing, much as it had rung when Baron Mantes split it open; perhaps such ringing never ceases, just grows fainter and returns. We are trapped in our worst moment forever, forever falling to the ground, falling . . .

He stood, his uncertain footsteps carrying him toward the tombstone, and he found himself staring at the amorphous shape above the skull, Christ crucified, the suffering features nearly obliterated by rain and wind. The cross was hung with spider webs, inside of which dark flies were suspended.

He bent at the fountain, splashed water on his face, fighting down the ugly fantasy that he was dead, that Lazare had tricked him, poisoned him, that he was nothing but a spectre haunting an alleyway. He knelt, removing his hat and ducking his whole head under. Good citizens, forgive, I'm a feverish traveler.

But the alleyway was empty, no one saw his bath. He

was alone, in a solitude which he suddenly felt to be complete, stretching endlessly across Europe, around the earth itself.

He walked on, holding his hat, leaving the alleyway behind. The tradesmen and office workers were finished for the day, and he asked a woman for directions. Her voice was empty, far off, like that of a woman met in a dream. He wanted to cry out, *Madame, we're dreamers, we're dreaming, you and I,* and she saw the madness in his eyes, turned quickly and walked away, leaving him standing on the street corner, beneath a statue of naked wrestling gods.

The insane asylum, then? The voice of the Viennese Chief mocked him with its suggestion, a suggestion that suddenly became a possibility. For how many, reflected Picard, how many grab their bars and scream, *This is a dream, let me free, I'm dreaming!*

He heard bright music ahead, aimed for it, seeking to be born into the world again, the everyday world of the street. An accordionist and guitar player stood at the edge of Am Hof Square, in which a festival of some sort was being held. He walked up to the musicians, tossed several coins into the battered hat they'd laid on the road. They nodded and continued playing, playing the world, playing life. They were older than he, the guitarist had only one leg, and played a cheerful tune of the street.

Picard moved against the building, leaned there, resting and listening. The guitarist too was leaning, his empty pinned-up pants leg fluttering in the wind. Picard tried to understand the words of the song, a folk song, something about *human, human, so nature has made us.*

A young boy appeared, running toward the musicians,

and he whispered to them, causing them to cease playing at once. Picard looked in the direction from which the boy had come.

A funeral cortege came toward them, the carriage draped in black, the horses pulling slowly. The coffin was a plain one, riding in a little hill of flowers that had been strewn in the carriage. The musicians had lowered their instruments, making them inconspicuous as the procession went on past. Only when the carriage had turned the distant corner beyond the square did they resume their tune: *human, human, so nature has made us.*

Picard's sombre mood dissolved as he entered Am Hof Square, finding it had been given over to a toy fair. The booths offered various enchantments—music boxes and banks, mechanical animals, farmyards, fortresses, oriental pagodas, miniature buildings of every kind. His childhood rose; he had lived in this magic land of dreaming toys, when Paris itself had been one of his toys. On the golden boulevard of memory he saw the secret of the lamps once more, that they were brightly dancing souls. A child's mind—the child sees all things as living—the streetlamps, the statues, and most of all his toys. His toys are living creatures. Ah god, what divine dreams.

He peered into a miniature townhouse, three stories high. In the cellar a tiny servant was reaching toward a wine rack. On the main floor a dinner party was in progress. The tiny women wore tiny gowns, the men perfectly tailored little tuxedos. The crowded parlor was supported by small Grecian pillars.

Picard nearly fell into the miniature gathering, removed himself with an apology to the creator of the dollhouse. It was of course only vaguely similar, was not Lazare's salon—one so easily projects an obsession. But the little figures are so well-made, so magically alive.

The next booth sold board games of every sort—in which dice were rolled and markers moved around wheels and squares, producing races between a shoe and a bell, a dog and a goat, other little objects which served to distinguish the players. We're on the wheel together, Lazare, somewhere through here. I know that I am near you.

He smiled at the elderly woman who ran the booth; she began speaking a dialect he couldn't follow. He nodded as if he understood, and picked up one of the markers—a silver hound which he moved toward a hare who was turning a corner of the board.

The woman rattled on, he thanked her and walked away, trying to remain clear and open to the influence, the hidden genie of the chase who was swirling and smoking in his bottle, seeking release.

Very well, come out, come enchant me, I know you're there, deep in my mind, know that you see what I cannot see. What is it?

At the next booth Noah's Ark sailed on a sea of glass; then a three-layered carousel turned, carrying a bright array of wooden animals. Picard felt his mind fuming with an insight, something perceived, yet not perceived.

"Wooden soldiers, sir? Something for your young lad —we've a marvelous cavalry here, and here the artillery . . ."

The toy seller moved the bright troops about, hauling cannon into place. Picard had to struggle against the fascinating little war staged before him, had to try and maintain himself as a student of the chase, rather than yield to the child who sought to live again in him, the lost boy of Parisian streets, the boy who'd played with such toys long ago, and wished to play with them again.

"No, no, thank you—but they are wonderful." These memories are sweet, but I have no need of you just now, little boy. Go away, go away . . .

He felt a tug in his heart, a sad little tug, as the boy dove back down into the darkness where he'd slumbered so long. Picard stood silent in the midst of the square, coldly observant, enchanted no longer, and still no wiser about Ric Lazare.

He circled the fair, through the flags and banners of fairyland which flew from the tops of the toy makers' tents. His mind was clear, with a discernment he wished were always his—every detail of the square seemed bathed in a mysterious light. I'm at the intersection of my case, I'm the fat wizard of toyland, but I don't see Lazare!

Where are you—you're hiding from me here, I'll bet all I own. The old hound knows a hare's track when he sniffs it.

The sun retired behind the stone walls of the city, and the toy makers lit their lamps. He was hungry, and nervous. Am I so stupid? It must be here, else why do I stay on, going in circles, like that mechanical duck there, on little red wheels.

But when he reached the edge of the square, he left the fair. Christmas is in the air, a special excitement reigns—perhaps that is all I'm feeling, the enchantment of the season. Self-deception is man's constant companion. Perhaps, after all, it is only the child in me who responds to the fair.

He turned back, looking through the stone canyon toward the lantern-lit square, and the attraction was intense, but of a sort he could not understand. He stood watching, staring into the fairy light, feeling that maybe the fairies had tricked him, as they were known to do. There had been men from the Prefecture swallowed up that way before—led clear around Europe on completely imagined scents. One took that sort of trip only once— the Prefect did not tolerate such expensive mistakes.

Picard found a coffeehouse, a bright, quiet place filled with Viennese reading their newspapers. He drank several coffees, and when the kitchen of the café began to emit pleasant smells he ordered supper, eating by the window, watching a faint mist move on the avenue. Toys still played in his head: the large stuffed bear of his childhood, whom he'd pounded hell out of. Poor bear, his head finally drooped, and the stuffing came out of his neck. I was a hard little bandit. But at night—at night I believe he lay beside me, faithful bear. Why do these thoughts keep coming; what do you see, child, what does little Paul have to tell me about Ric Lazare?

From the mist, two dark-haired gypsy children appeared, a boy and a girl, walking toward the café door, flowers in their arms. Picard's seat was closest to the door, and they came straight to him.

"Flowers, sir? Flowers for your girl?"

Picard smiled, started to reach for a coin, but the owner of the café came quickly forward, scolding the children and chasing them out the door. He returned to Picard's table, apologetically. "I'm sorry they bothered you, sir. They steal the flowers from the cemetery . . ."

The owner smiled then, his gesture concluded, and walked away. Picard turned back to the window, a feeling of cold moving through him, despite the hot wine he'd been sipping. The gypsy children were walking on through the mist; he rose from the table and paid his check. Merest chance that they should have chosen me with their death flowers. Merest chance. Third token of death today. He stepped into the street. The evening had grown milder, the cold edge gone and the mist getting thicker. As he walked, the piping of the child came to him again, the ghost of memory haunting his footsteps. He felt his childhood, his toys, as if he were still carrying them along with him in a sack—Jack the jester who popped out of a box, and a monkey who hung on a string.

Childhood, the past—go deeper into Lazare's past, find his origins, certainly, if only I knew where to look. Which city, where . . .

He was attracted to the sign of the Elyseum ballroom, whose lobby was decorated with junk from various parts of Europe and the world. He descended, into the dance. The room was enormous; there was a French section, a South American, an African; other geographical niches glittered beyond these, and he moved slowly through the crowd. Tables ringed the dance floor and everyone was drunk. The lamps wore shades of many colors, the floor was smooth as a skating rink, shining with reflected light, in which he saw his hulking form. He ignored the suggestion in his footsteps, the nagging and monstrous suggestion that he was a mere shadow crossing the floor, and less than shadow, a creature of mist doomed to be scattered by the sun.

"Yes, a brandy, please."

The music had ceased and the musicians were themselves taking fortification; other gentlemen were leaning at the bar, or gathered in the doorways. He occupied himself with the sight of the ladies, called for another brandy, and mused on the strange sensation of unreality that now seemed to be his constant companion—old age creeping up on me, perhaps. But there is one sure antidote for that poison, and you, voluptuous Fräulein, are it.

He stepped from the bar, and as he did so she looked away, though but a moment before her gaze had been spinning its way toward him, spinning softly, with silken suggestiveness, promising to wrap him in gently, to change him from a wretched worm to a butterfly, for a moment at least.

Her hair was golden, the gold bangles on her wrists glittering as she arranged a lock of hair over her ear and delicately brought her hand down in front of her, still pretending she didn't see him approaching. The shape of her fingernails seemed to have claimed her full attention.

— ⁓ ⁓ —

Her gown—black lace ribboned with the German tri-color of black, red, and gold—lay upon the floor. She stood in the middle of the room, removing her black stockings. Her legs were marvelous, slightly muscled in the calves, legs of a dancer, and she had the belly of a girl who loves her beer, a girl after my own tastes, thought Picard, taking her in his arms.

She straightened, her stockings only half off, and gave him a deep wet kiss, lolling her tongue around in his mouth as he patted her gorgeous big heinie.

"You have a liking for it, yes?" she whispered in school-girl French, and he answered in equally clumsy German that indeed he had a liking for it, in fact would like to own it.

They stumbled toward the bed, his jacket and pants falling along the way. She mixed her kisses with other languid attempts at French, making each hesitant word a further intimacy, as she unbuttoned his undershorts, pulled them away, slipped her fingers beneath his undershirt, pulled it away, asking what brought him to Vienna and learning that he was a balloon enthusiast, come for a fair.

A distant church bell struck the late hour. Through the window they heard the street watchman tapping the lampposts and singing his lonely verse, which she translated slowly for Picard, punctuating it with long searching kisses, her whisper blending with the watchman's gruff warning:

> "*Good people all, I pray take care*
> *And speedily to bed repair*
> *For midnight arrives, the day expires*
> *So shut your door and quench your fires.*"

"We've repaired to bed," said Picard, caressing her huge breasts.

"Yes," she said gently, "and now you'll quench my fire."

When he left the room, she was sleeping, and he went quietly down the steps of her building to the street, where the night watchman was again passing in his grey frock coat, wearing a large tin hat and black garters. His pole was long and tipped with iron, and he looked Picard over carefully, speaking a caution.

"I'm speeding toward bed," answered Picard with a beatific smile, and the policeman understood that this lover was no threat to the night. He passed on, lightly tapping his pole, and Picard went in the opposite direction, toward his hotel. Once more as he walked he felt the presence of the fairy child in him, a sliver of moonlight in his soul, haunting and distant. And with it he suddenly heard the mocking voice of Ric Lazare, saying, *It is only a toy, monsieur.*

T H E morning was grey, his cape windblown, and scattered snowflakes fell on the booths and stalls of the toy makers. But despite the cold, the atmosphere was warm, the booths all heated by small stoves or open braziers, and the toys performed as usual on the counters and tables—dancing, drumming, opening and closing their eyes, making soft cries or squeals of delight when moved by the toy makers' hands.

"I saw a toy once, a very elaborate one; it was a machine that clicked out one's fortune."

"If it's fortune you're after, sir, here is my husband's version of the House of Wealth—a bank that takes your money in the most delightful way. Have you a coin?"

Picard gave the woman a coin, which she deposited in the mouth of a tin dog, who stood upon a metal platform, beside a tin doghouse. The woman touched the dog's tail and he moved along a groove to the house, where he deposited the coin through a slot in the roof. It clinked away, out of sight, and Picard moved too, toward another booth, where a dancing toy bear was turning. The toy maker was a young man, smiling, wearing a long scarf around his neck, and warming his fingers over his brazier.

"Have you ever seen a toy that told fortunes?"

"No, sir, I've not," said the young man. "There's precious little fortune in toys, I'll tell you."

"You must work long hours on them."

"As a hobby, sir. To pass the time, after working seventy hours a week in the factory."

Picard moved on, from booth to booth, inquiring after a fortune-telling toy that clicked like a telegraph machine. The snow continued to whirl; no one had seen such a toy; indeed, it didn't even sound like a toy. "If you want a toy, sir, a real toy, look here, at this kangaroo . . ."

He stood in the middle of the square, with the medieval-like booths all around him, their many flags and banners whipping in the wind. The feeling was strange, as if he'd known it all before, long ago, on the jousting field of a bygone age. He smiled to himself, recognizing the enchantment of the toys again, which filled the mind with fairy tales.

He stared up and down the rows of the toy makers, making certain that he'd inquired at every booth. He heard the embattled voice of two of the toy makers, somewhere toward the fringe of the fair grounds. While he could not quickly translate the shouts, he understood the universal language of resentment, especially when it is joined by the wife of one of the combatants, as now seemed to have happened. He caught sight of the contest, between one booth, already set up, whose owners, a man and a woman, were screaming at a bent little pin of a man, who was, with the help of an obviously dim-witted youth, trying to set up his own tent. Despite the scolding of his neighbors, he continued setting up shop, and smiled at the approach of Picard.

"Having trouble?" asked Picard, answering the bent man's smile.

"None at all, sir," said the bent man, as if the storm of protest were not falling on his head. Then, turning to the boy: "Hurry up there, lad, we've got a visitor."

Picard assisted the dim-witted youth in the securing of the tent pole, which brought a hiss from the neighbor woman and a grunt of disgust from her husband.

"All right, sir, we'll just be a moment," said the bent man. He lit a lantern and opened his trunk, withdrawing a number of conventional toys—little hopping rabbits, birds who chirped when wound, and a fish on wheels.

"I'm looking for an unusual toy, not the sort of thing I've seen anywhere around here," said Picard.

"Of course," said the bent man, "a discerning collector. Of course, my dear sir, I have exactly what you're looking for." He signaled to the dim-witted young man, who lifted a second trunk onto the toy maker's bench. The bent man opened it and withdrew a toy man, clothed in a barrel. "Now here is a somewhat unusual . . ." He lifted the barrel over the man's head, and in so doing exposed the man's miniature sexual member, which rose up quickly to erection, supported by a rubber spring. The peddler lowered the barrel again, covering the man's private parts. "A novelty." He smiled. "A comic piece. . . . Here we have something for your tree . . ."

He brought out a large Christmas ball, beautifully made,

wreathed with bright bands and bits of sparkle. Handing it to Picard, he said, "Look closely, sir. Yes, Father Christmas has come . . ."

Picard held up the Christmas ball. On one side of it was a tiny glass window. He peeked through it, into the interior of the ball, where a tiny naked lady lay, upon a tiny bed, with Father Christmas atop her, delivering his gift.

"Yes," said the bent man, taking back the ball, "just a touch of cheer, for the holiday season, you see . . . now, let me . . ." He dug in his trunk again, like Father Christmas himself, mumbling amongst his gifts.

"I'm looking for a fortune-telling machine," said Picard. "One which clicks out information of a very special kind . . ."

"You've seen the work of Robert Heron, then."

"Robert Heron?"

"My dear sir, who else could make such a thing as you describe. Surely none of these jackasses!" The bent man gestured toward the other booths in the fair.

"Who is Robert Heron?"

"The greatest toy maker in the world."

"Where may I find him?"

"His home is in Nuremberg."

"And he makes a fortune-telling toy?"

"His automatic mechanisms are without peer. I daresay his toys can do what angels cannot."

There was a scuffling outside the tent, and the door was suddenly filled by a grey-frocked policeman and the wife of the next-door toy maker. The woman was still red-faced with indignation and the policeman came forward, spurred on by her loud protestations.

"Who is the owner of this tent?"

"I am," said the bent man.

"I understand that obscene objects are for sale here, which is strictly against the law. I must ask you, sir, to . . ."

"Excuse me," said Picard, opening his wallet and showing his credentials, as well as the special visitor's badge issued him by the Viennese Chief of Police.

"Yes, sir," said the policeman. "May I be of assistance?"

"I'm working with your Chief," said Picard, "and this man is helping me in my investigation. I would appreciate it if his perfectly innocent display of toys"— Picard gestured toward a tricycling goat—"be left unmolested. He is of great service to me."

"Very good, sir," said the policeman. Turning to the dumbfounded woman, he gestured toward her with his walking stick and directed her out of the tent. At the last moment, he leaned back in and touched his hat with his fingers. "Don't worry, gentlemen, there'll be no further interruptions." He disappeared, then, and the next-door neighbors were silenced.

"Thank you," said the bent man.

"Robert Heron is in Nuremberg, you say?"

"He was when last I saw him, nearly a year ago."

Picard adjusted the collar of his cape and took hold of the tent flap. "I'm grateful for your help." He moved the tent flap aside, but then turned back, drawn to a toy the idiot assistant was placing on the wooden display bench.

"You like it, sir?" asked the bent man. "You may have it."

Picard picked up the glass ball. It was clear glass, and constructed within it were a few tiny buildings and a man pulling a cart beside them, through a layer of snow which covered the bottom of the ball. He shook the ball and the snowflakes rose up, suspended in water, and slowly fell around the rooftops and onto the man's head. Picard watched them fall, a peculiar feeling coming over him, as if he knew the figure in the glass, had known him for many years, indeed for all time.

"A beautiful thing," said Picard, setting the ball back onto the bench.

"Worlds within worlds, sir. I have here another transparent glass, the subject of which is somewhat more sophisticated, Miss Schmidt and the Delivery Boy, for private collectors only . . ." He reached into his other trunk, but Picard was already departing the tent, into the blowing storm.

T H E train was halted by drifting dunes of snow. Picard left his compartment and walked to the end of the coach. The conductor shook his head; there was no telling when the tracks would be cleared. "We're not far from the inn, if you care to walk." He pointed toward a curl of smoke that played among the falling snowflakes. "You can hire a carriage from there."

Picard returned to his compartment and picked up his bag. Other passengers were doing the same. They stepped from the train, into the knee-deep snow. The snowflakes fell upon his face, and he raised his footsteps high, drinking in the fresh clean draughts of winter air. Nuremberg can't be more than an hour's ride; up this hill, then, that's a stout lad, push your fat along and don't eat so much today.

The road to the inn was being plowed by a team of men and horses, who dragged a large wooden blade

through the snow. The horses' manes were filled with
snow and the men's beards glistened with frost. They'd
obviously been working all night, for the way was now
wide enough for a carriage sled to pass through easily.
Picard entered the inn with four other passengers and
they engaged the carriage for immediate departure.

The horses were fresh, shivering and stamping in their
harness, eager to be moving. Picard tossed his luggage on
top and settled in by the window, joined by an elderly
man and his wife, and two young women, apparently of
the teaching profession, for they had taken out a text-
book and were sharing it on their laps. Picard considered
opening the book he had in his own coat pocket, then
decided against it. The memoirs of Celeste Savidant bore
a rather lurid cover and might prove upsetting to the
young women, and perhaps to the old boy and his wife.
It was the sort of reading matter Picard liked, but not
now; a trifle inappropriate. Just relax and watch the
scenery.

"You're going to Nuremberg, sir?" asked the old man.
Picard nodded.

"On business, yes?"

"I'm a toy collector," said Picard.

"Ah, I see," said the old man. His wife, a shy little
Frau, whispered in her husband's ear, and he smiled,
nodding toward Picard. "Yes, if you're a collector, you
must see our friend Hermann Wilderstein. He lives in the
shadow of the great Tower. I'll write down the address
for you."

"I'm very grateful," said Picard. "Is Herr Wilderstein
a collector?"

"A toy maker. An excellent one."

"Are you familiar with the work of Robert Heron?"

"Naturally. He is the finest in the world."

"Do you know him?"

"I've seen him about. You'll find his shop. It's near the . . . isn't it near the Hauptmarkt, mama?"

The old woman nodded her head and smiled at Picard. Her husband, now satisfied of the stranger's business, closed his eyes and folded his hands across his stomach. The two young women continued their lesson, in mathematics, and Picard turned toward the window. He'd been flung out of school as a boy, mathematics being only one of the things about which he had no understanding, or interest, and their voices brought back all his old feelings of insecurity, as if the lesson were being prepared for him, for the stout, stupid little Picard, hiding in the last row.

The runners of the sleigh cut along through the snow with a softly hissing sound, and Picard took refuge in it, forgetting all voices, from the present and the past. Snow-laden trees bent low over the road, and the horses gave off a subtle perfume, the scent of vigor, of strength. Cottages appeared, fell away behind them; the old man snored quietly, and Picard looked toward the next bit of firelight and smoke, where a house and barn were nestled at the edge of the forest. The cows were standing outside the barn, and had made a tangle of paths all around it, through the snow. The farmer who'd just milked them had loaded his wagon with milk cans and was bringing it toward the road.

The moment froze, a cheap Christmas calendar, an innocuous winterland scene become the quintessence of

horror to Picard, who stared dumbfounded at each suspended detail: the smoke held in the air, unmoving, the
farmer and his horse immobile as two wooden toys.

"That is for Nuremberg," said the old woman softly,
destroying the spell, setting free the smoke, the farmer,
the horse, and Picard, whose heart began beating again.
The old man muttered in his sleep, and she touched his
sleeve. He woke, looked around him in puzzlement for
a moment, then smiled at Picard.

"Your toys, sir, do they bring a good price in other
parts of Europe?"

"Depending on who has made them," said Picard nervously, looking out the window, turning back to be sure
the farmer and his horse did not again become creatures
of ice. He faced the old man, tried to smile. "The toys of
Robert Heron . . ."

"Of course, they'll fetch the best price, as well they
should. A remarkable craftsman."

"I've heard he even makes a fortune-telling machine."

"I've never seen it, but I can tell you this—old Heron
knows a thing or two. He's a strange fellow, Heron is. A
trifle mad, yes?"

The old woman shook her head no, and clucked her
tongue in disapproval. Her husband cleared his throat,
changed his tone. "You're right, mama, old Heron isn't
mad. He's—a visionary. Yes, that's the better word. Old
Heron is a visionary. His father was the same way; a
watchmaker, but what a watchmaker! He built a clock—
you should have seen it, sir—a clock that had angels
circling on it, and peculiar little animals, and there were
entrances and exits and hallways in this clock. It was

enormous, bigger than two men, and as the hands went round the various figures danced, synchronized with the hands of time. It was in the town hall for years and then —then, I think it was presented as a gift to a visiting king. Anyway, sir, you see what I mean—Robert Heron came by his gift honestly, for his father was one of our city's great masters."

The old man turned toward the window. More houses had appeared, and other sleighs were moving on the side roads, and on the main road. The spires of a cathedral appeared in the distance, rising out of the storm. Then the clouds parted for a moment and thousands of snow-capped roofs could be seen.

"There is the Tower," said the old man, pointing to the ancient castle that sat upon the rock heights of Nuremberg. "Herr Wilderstein lives just next to it. You will find him most hospitable."

The huge rock walls of the city loomed up, snow-covered, silent, unmanned; the city was at peace. The sled entered with many others, and fell in behind a brewer's wagon, which bore its barrels of beer undeterred by the storm. On the sidewalks, the shopkeepers were shoveling out side by side with home owners. The windows of the restaurants and beer gardens were only just beginning to lose their frosty designs as inner fires warmed them, and children pummeled the passing sleds with snowballs, one of which crashed against the glass just beyond Picard's face. He started, saw the answer to the entire case, and lost it. His mind raced frantically, seeking to overtake the half-formed intuition, but it was gone, back into the land of shadows, leaving him with only a single impression, of glass which must shatter—a breaking bottle on a ship's bow, a window broken by stones, a crystal ball flung against the wall.

"There is a hotel on the next corner," said the old man. "You won't be uncomfortable there. Not too expensive either."

Picard rapped on the driver's window, and the sled was drawn over to the doorway of the hotel. A servant came immediately and received Picard's luggage. The old man leaned out the window. "I trust you'll find the toys you seek. If I can find any old ones in my attic I'll send them round to you . . . Ah no, mama says I cannot. We must hang on to them for the grandchildren. So—there's the value . . . goodbye then . . ."

The hotel staff was still shoveling, and Picard watched them from his window as he changed into his Norfolk jacket. The knickerbocker trousers, ending just below the knee, would make snow-walking easier. The socks were thick, would turn the water.

He tugged on the tweed cap he always wore with the Norfolk, an Irish creation whose brim had been bent through the years into a smoothly rounded arch. Fastening the belt of his jacket, he observed with some pleasure that it closed one notch tighter. Traveling has taken off some of the spread; let me just check this . . .

The Lefaucheux revolver came open with a click, he examined the chamber, blew a minute particle of dust out of it, and returned it to his jacket. He was feeling strong, exhilarated by the blowing weather, walked down the stairs and through the lobby, into the wind, the close-fitting Norfolk suit having the feel of a uniform as he strode into the snowy street.

He walked toward the center of the city, following the slope of the gentle valley on which the town had been built. A postman was coming toward him, shouldering his letter bag. Picard stopped the man, inquired for the house of Robert Heron.

"Henkersteg," said the postman, pointing toward a succession of small wooden bridges. Picard continued down the sloping street and turned in the direction the postman had pointed, along the narrow little stream that flowed through the fairy-tale city. The small gently arching bridges spanned it, one after another, as in a matchbox Paris with a miniature Seine.

Henkersteg, the Hangman's Bridge: Picard located it on his map and then with his eye, a humble bridge like all the others which crossed the little stream, except that here men had dangled over the water at the end of a rope. Not an ordinary bridge, mein Herr, not ordinary at all. A bridge leading across a vast and unknown water, to places only the hanged men know. And leading as well to a row of shabby houses on the water, one of which is Robert Heron's.

The porches were built over the water, supported by long naked poles; the dooryards were a jumble of rotted shingles and trash barrels, and stiffened wash hung on the open porches. Picard circled around to the front of the row houses, finding the door of Robert Heron at once— the frame was carved into an arbor, with faces of gnomes and elves peeking from the leaves, mischievous smiles on their faces. He took hold of the brass knocker and rapped solidly.

Receiving no answer, he rapped again. Footsteps slowly approached from inside, and the door opened. An old woman stood before him, her body frail and white as a porcelain doll.

"I'm looking for Robert Heron," said Picard.

"He's dead."

"Dead? When did he die?"

The woman looked at him, hesitation in her eyes. "Who are you?"

"I'm from the Paris police," said Picard, showing his shield.

"Very well," said the woman. "But come inside. We're letting the cold in, and it's cold enough."

He followed her to her parlor, where she sat down in a rocking chair beside a window, looking out onto Hangman's Bridge. "He died two months ago," she said, slowly rocking back and forth, staring at the celebrated bridge.

"How did he die?"

"In a ring of broken toys." Robert Heron's widow was a small woman, made still smaller by old age, her feet hardly touching the floor as she rocked, a withered doll who rocked through a secret eternity.

"A ring of toys? I don't understand."

"He gathered all his toys around him and smashed them one by one," said the woman, without emotion. "They were the most wonderful toys on earth, and after he smashed them to bits, he lay down and died amongst them."

Picard sat in silence with Heron's widow, she seeming not to care if he sat there forever.

"Did your husband have any assistants?"

"No."

"No apprentice, no pupils in the art?"

"He worked alone. Only he knew the secret of his toys, and he took it with him." The old woman pointed to a door. Picard went to it and entered the toy maker's studio. On the floor was a pile of broken springs and wires and wheels and tiny arms and legs and lovely heads and torsos. He knelt before the ruin of little bodies, touching them gently with his fingertips. The sadness of his childhood overtook him again, and he stood, not wishing to open that wound. But the sunlight moved, extending a beam into the heart of the scattered toy kingdom, where a bit of sequin suddenly glittered. Picard knelt again, drawn to the sparkling waistband of a circus acrobat, in white and black tights, with gold cincher and wristbands. The acrobat had somehow been spared in the final destruction of the toys. Picard picked the figure out of the fragments. Then, looking closely at the face, he felt a sudden vertigo, as if he were the acrobat, falling from the high wire into a bottomless abyss. The face on the toy was that of Ric Lazare.

 ⌒⌒⌒

He stood upon a sheltered wooden bridge, staring at the stream below. Snow was still falling, touching the water for a moment and disappearing. He reached into his pocket and withdrew the circus acrobat. While he was not in the habit of stealing from old women, it could not be helped; when the case is over, I'll send it back to her, wrapped in an appreciative note from the Prefecture and lined with German marks.

The acrobat was perfectly made; a tiny key was folded almost invisibly in his back. *I hold Lazare; he has been in Nuremberg.*

Picard wound the key a few turns, and released it. The acrobat squirmed in his hands, arms and legs kicking powerfully, but unable to go anywhere.

Picard smiled and returned the acrobat to his pocket. He continued across the bridge, toward a promontory of land on which a weeping willow drooped over the water. *Were I to be hanged in Nuremberg, I would choose this bridge, for the sight of the willow as I dangled.*

He walked past the tree, and into a street that rose sharply upward to the northwest, toward Castle Rock, the pinnacle of the city's skyline. It was a long, slow climb, through ever-narrowing lanes and up stone steps. He huffed onto Am Ölberg, the winding street that lay in the shadow of the great Tower. At number 31, he rapped on the door of Hermann Wilderstein, toy maker.

❧

"No," said Wilderstein, "there were no assistants, nor an apprentice." The toy maker was plump, red-faced, a good solid burgher, whose house was as carefully made and as highly polished as his toys, every latch and doorframe a masterpiece of care and craftsmanship. "Many young lads were sent to him, but Heron insisted they have complete knowledge of anatomy and geometry. May I bring you a glass of brandy, sir, you look quite pale."

"No," said Picard, "the hill has tired me, it is nothing serious, please go on."

The toy maker called his serving girl and had the brandy brought anyway, taking one himself as he continued his reflections on the work of Robert Heron: "Yes, anatomy and geometry, and the processes of nature. In all this he was adamant. The proper making of toys could not begin without such knowledge already in the mind. His own guidebook was that of our most famous artist, Albrecht Dürer. Do you know Dürer's *Instruction in Measuring with the Compass and Ruler*? A marvelous book. There was also his work on human proportion. Heron lived by these books, and expected anyone who wanted to learn the art to have such knowledge. Well, I ask you, sir, what young lad is going to come up out of nowhere with such learning at his disposal? Or, if he did have such learning, he would go on to be a painter or sculptor, where he might make a good deal more fame for himself." The burgher finished his brandy, stared into the empty glass. "So Robert Heron's superb gift was not passed on, and we'll never see the likes of it again. My favorite was his miniature city: It was entirely animated. The cows walked along each morning toward their pasture, and at lunchtime the tiny church bells rang; in the evening the night watchman made his rounds, and a drunkard reeled down the street. It went continually as if everyone in it were animated by—by life. Its secret, of course, was a magnificent system of springs and balances whose intricacies would drive most men mad."

Picard withdrew the acrobat from his pocket, and before he could say a word, Hermann Wilderstein had reached forth his hand.

"Ah, sir, how fortunate you are! This is a priceless find, priceless . . ." Wilderstein turned the acrobat over in his hands, examining every detail of it, holding it as one holds a sacred child. Finally he set it down on the coffee table, shaking his head affectionately. "And how much do you want for it?"

"I'm not interested in selling."

"Quite right, quite. Keep it always, and it will bring you good luck, for I swear to you, sir, his toys are all enchanted, and this . . ." Wilderstein picked it up again, wound the key gently. "This is one of his best. Look at the detail, and now look . . . look at the action!" He set the acrobat down and the little figure performed a perfect run of somersaults, the steel-veined arms and legs carrying him end over end, across the floor. He finished upright, poised, ready to be wound again. Picard reached down to the acrobat and picked him up, setting him on the coffee table, where he stood frozen, silent, yet somehow more alive than ever.

"Do you know who the model for this was, Herr Wilderstein?"

Wilderstein looked at the face of the acrobat. "It's one of a circus set he worked on for many years. Heron had an entire circus, you know, waltzing elephants, high-wire acts, all in miniature. The model for this could have been any one of a number of circus performers. Heron loved the circus, and always attended when the tents were erected in Nuremberg. I saw him there, many times, and he was continually sketching faces and details of the performance. I expect . . ." Herr Wilderstein touched the acrobat on the head. ". . . this fellow was part of some passing troupe."

Picard stood, putting the acrobat back in his pocket. "Thank you for your time, Herr Wilderstein."

"It was nothing, sir. It's always a pleasure to meet a serious collector." Herr Wilderstein showed Picard toward the door of the old house.

"Where is Robert Heron buried?"

"In the cemetery of St. John. In that direction . . ." Herr Wilderstein stepped with Picard into the street, pointing toward the end of it. "You must cross the wall and then it is straight on from there. But the gates have closed now . . ." He took out his pocket watch. "Yes, you're too late. Tomorrow, sir, try again tomorrow."

Picard gave the toy maker a last salute and walked on down Am Ölberg, with the shadows of evening fast approaching.

He found a tavern for dinner, noisy with the music of a Tyrolean band, and famous, so the menu said, for its flaming pancake. He drank a bit of dark beer, but only picked at his food, for his attention was wholly taken up by the little circus acrobat he'd set on the table. The figure stood arrogantly beside a pitcher of beer and a half-empty glass, his hands on his hips, waiting for his spring to command him.

You're troubled by feelings of mediocrity, said the gypsy woman in Picard's mind, and he was forced to acknowledge that it was true. The miniature replica of Ric Lazare exercised a certain force over him, exuding, as did Lazare, cleverness and confidence. Lazare is a man of dash, a brilliant performer on the heights of Paris, and his little puppet is just like him—poised, glittering, audacious.

While I am a bloodhound, faithful and predictable. But nonetheless, Monsieur Lazare, I am on your trail, barking at your heels.

Picard pocketed the acrobat and left the tavern, his body as restless as his mind. The night sky was clear, ruled by a full moon which intensified the white veil of the city. He walked aimlessly, from street corner to corner, drawn by nothing more compelling than the shadow of a lamppost on the snow. Coming to a wooded park at the edge of the city, he entered it, and found a skaters' rink. The ice was lit by lamps and lanterns and a crowd of skaters was playing rink tennis. The women's long dresses were pinned up in sweeping folds that freed their skates from entanglement and they glided gracefully to and fro before the net.

He stood at the edge of the rink, leaning on a wooden railing. The mood of the ice was utterly romantic, and he surrendered to its soft light, as the skaters played, and laughed, and clutched each other suddenly, to keep from falling. Carriages pulled up through the trees, landing more enthusiasts at the rink, all of whom soon laced their skates and entered onto the moonstruck mirror. Some played ice tennis, others went through dance maneuvers, and some went alone, off on speedy revolutions around the outermost edge. Yet all who were on that mirror, no matter what design their skates cut into its surface, were fabulous beings enjoying special privileges of love. For it's clear—love has brought them here, love in all its forms; something about the ice at night, the snowy perimeter and the silently watching trees—a paradise for lovers. Even those young men who skate swiftly by themselves, who treat with disdain any lady less swift than they—even those young men are circling through dreams of love.

Beyond the mirror, on the snowy hills which curved around the circular rink in billowing rolls, couples were sledding, holding tightly to each other, embracing through heavy clothing, cold and muffled embraces which none-theless must burn with intense heat. For Picard remem-bered—a snowy hill in Paris many years ago—he and a young lady on a sled, going downhill from Montmartre, all promise and hope; they'd walked slowly through the streets, pulling the sled together, hurrying toward the fulfillment of the promise. The fulfillment was forgotten, like many other similar moments, but the sleigh ride lived on in his heart, on and on, downhill with you, darling, girl of my youth, downhill with you, the wind upon your hair and I touch your breasts through the rough wool of your coat.

He walked slowly around the rink, stopped beside a young couple—she seated on a log bench, he lacing her skates. Picard smiled on love, as only an old and battered lover can, with a knowing smile; she'll take him round the ice, though he thinks that he is taking her; and afterward they'll sip hot wine beside a fire and she'll take him round her finger, round and round, while he believes throughout that he is taking her with his boasts, his leaps, his courage, his all. And all along it's the moon who rules, my friends, love's power is beyond you both.

Picard walked on, suffused with that part of love given to those who watch from the sidelines, an ever-expanding feeling, the embrace of a lonely lover who embraces the whole night—its lamps, its skaters, its steaming wine.

He put the rink behind him and walked slowly toward the place where the carriages were turning. One was turning there now, and stopping. Picard saw a pretty face at the window, and then the door was opened by a coachman and she descended, in a green bolero jacket and pinned-up skirt of red wool, her blond curls topped by a round little hat with a feather in it. She was a lovely creature, petite, but with an aristocratic haughtiness quite charming in one so small. He knew that she would make mincemeat of her companion's heart before the night was out; and here was the fortunate gentleman now, coming around beside the horses, his caped figure entrapped by shadows for the moment, but Picard felt for him, whoever he was. Picard moved closer, his smile touching the couple momentarily, and then suddenly changing as the gentleman's shadowy face was caught by the moon. His eyes met Picard's; he raised his cane straight before him.

Picard had already drawn his revolver, his motion swifter than the swiftest skater on the ice that night, as he discharged a fire flash toward the ivory satin waistcoat of Baron Mantes.

The Baron's pistol-cane returned the fire—Picard saw the bullet leap from the highly polished tip of the cane, but it had been too hastily aimed, going past Picard's head and traveling into the trees. The Baron smiled elegantly even as Picard's bullet entered his chest, and his ivory waistcoat burst into red.

The young woman brought her hand to her mouth, stifling a scream. The Baron, dropping his cane and turning slowly toward her, tried to execute a last bow. His knees betrayed him, and he crumbled before her, his top hat falling in the snow and his handsome chiseled face coming to rest on her black shoe tip. His eyes were open and he was unquestionably dead.

She fell upon him, weeping. A crowd quickly gathered, but kept their distance. Picard still held the smoking revolver, lowering it only very slowly, his body enjoying a luxurious warp, his musculature controlled down to the most minute detail.

The young woman's sobs brought an end to the delicate tremor in his nerves, and it was with annoyance that he looked down at her, annoyance which immediately changed to gentle concern, for her eyes were filled with love's ruin.

He reached into his wallet, producing his identification. "I am Inspector Picard of the Paris Prefecture. Your companion is a well-known murderer, responsible for the death of at least nine women. I assure you, he would have . . ."

Her eyes fired at him, releasing black balls of hatred which left no trace upon his skin but dove deep into his spirit. "You are the murderer!" she screamed. "You've murdered my love . . . you . . . you . . ." Her expletive was strangled in hatred and sorrow and she fell once again upon the stiffening Baron, covering his bluish cheeks with her tears.

Picard stood awkwardly by, aware of the insult he'd given to the night, here at the mirror of love, where blood was dripping slowly from the Baron's heart onto the pure white snow. Every lover, every skater, was now certainly in shock; coldness had come over their embrace, a coldness that would not yield, not for a long while. Only later, much later in the night, would the bravest of them be able to lie together. For death—Picard saw it moving everywhere now, amongst the skaters, by the carriages, in the fluttering capes of the approaching policemen— death was the highest ruler of the night.

T H E morning was bright, the sky clear. He sat in the dining room of the hotel, scribbling a message; a waiter stood nearby, ready to send it to the telegraph office. Picard looked it over one last time:

Nailed Mantes Nuremberg—have Lazare's trail—Picard

He summoned the waiter and handed him the paper. "It must go out at once."

"It will, Inspector, without fail."

He returned to his breakfast, finishing his roll and coffee. Sunlight streamed across the table, playing upon the iron handle of Baron Mantes's pistol-cane, which leaned against the table's edge. *You wish it as a souvenir, monsieur? Of course, of course.* The Nuremberg police were very kind.

He reached for it now, examining it more closely—Remington, .32 calibre. He had an immediate affection for the piece, rubbed the ball and claw handle lightly on the bridge of his nose, where the Baron had once so forcefully laid it. And where did the Baron find you, what tales are yours, little brother?

Upon the ball he saw eleven tiny scratches side by side, etched into the iron. He took out his pocketknife and added a twelfth line.

❧

The entrance to the St. John cemetery was marked by a stone house, and the attendant who answered the door seemed to have lately crawled from the grave—an old man with eyes expressionless as marbles. Picard received instructions to the grave of Robert Heron, and threaded his way along a snow-laden aisle. On all sides elaborate stone sepulchres marked the snowfield. Robert Heron's grave was marked by a slab of stone only; the snow had been cleared away by a gloved hand. A low juniper shrub had been uncovered and around it childlike little paths had been dug and tiny walls of snow erected, so as to form a miniature courtyard. Picard looked at the footprints beside the grave—small like a child's, and from the cut and impress of the heel surely a male.

He followed the footprints through the graveyard, back to the entrance gate, and knocked again at the door of the caretaker.

"Who has been tending Robert Heron's grave?"

"Appel Meisterlin, of Holy Ghost Almhouse."

"Robert Heron was a saint, my friend," said Appel Meisterlin. "He'd found the deepest secrets of nature and he manifested them in his toys. They had . . ." The old man stared out a high frost-covered window of the alms-house. ". . . little souls."

"No one else knew these secrets?"

"Now that's a strange tale," said Appel Meisterlin. "Might we pursue it further over some soup with noodles? There's a café down the block, if you would be my guest . . ."

The pauper led the way to a restaurant, where Picard ordered a full-scale meal for himself and Appel Meisterlin. The old man dunked his bread in the soup, and talked between mouthfuls.

"We often traveled together to the toy fairs, Heron and I, for though I wasn't his equal as a toy maker we got along well enough to make such journeys pleasant. I learned, sir, I drank deeply from that great man's spirit, giving in return the bit of understanding which a lonely genius like Heron needed, for at times he confessed to feeling that he'd gone completely out of the world of men, into the enchanted regions of the toys. *They aren't like men*, he would say to me. *They are much finer than men, and much worse.* I never quite understood what he meant, but I knew he was grappling with a philosophical problem of great importance to him. From hints he let drop, I gathered that he considered his toys capable of working both good and evil."

"Was there an apprentice?"

The old man's fingers closed with difficulty around the coffee cup. He brought it slowly to his lips, and slowly set it back down. "Heron and I were in the Town Park in Buda, at the end of the long road from the inner city. We were old hands at that fair, having exhibited there since the park was first constructed. But the time I'm speaking of is not so far back, oh, maybe twenty years or so ago. We had been showing for several days when a young man came, carrying a toy that he had made—a marching soldier, beautifully carved and mechanically perfect. Heron was amazed. I'd never seen him so impressed by the work of another man. At first he was critical of the young man's work and only I, who knew him, could see that he had at last received the apprentice he'd been waiting for. He'd often talked about this forthcoming apprentice. *The toys have told me*, he said. *I will have an apprentice.* But no, *apprentice* was not the word he used. It was *disciple.* You see? There is a difference. It was a matter of deep faith, Robert Heron's genius, and that night after the fair was over he was almost beside himself with joy. *At last*, he said, *here is the man who has the touch.*"

"It was a young man?"

"A lad of about fifteen, I'd say, but very mature in his ways, strangely so, as if there were within him—an old man. I was continually fascinated by this aspect of his nature, and Heron told me that it was the toys which had given the look of old age to the lad's eyes, that the toys themselves were age-old."

"Where was this young man from?"

"A place along the Danube, a strange name, I have not forgotten it. Robert Heron's disciple was from the valley called Deep Sorrow."

"Did you ever visit this valley?"

"There is a lake there, quite beautiful. Unfortunately, the disciple was deep sorrow for Robert Heron."

"How so? . . . Waiter, bring us dessert, please."

"He was every bit as talented as Heron himself. I saw that after only a few days. His technical abilities were quite past my comprehension. He and Heron would talk of mechanical rules that were foreign language to me. The lad brought other toys he'd made, opened them up for us. Intricately designed, sir, born of that intense fascination which allows a man to go ever deeper into the secret of the craft. I had no such gift; my patience would dissolve, my hand tremble, and I'd sleep. But Heron and his disciple would work long into the night, manufacturing gears so tiny you could hardly see them with the naked eye. And then dropped those gears into place with a tweezers, with a prayer, with god knows what kind of strange passion . . ." The pauper stirred his coffee thoughtfully, slowly round and round. "During the weeks of that fair, they made a lute player, whose miniature instrument could be perfectly tuned. More astonishing— the wooden fingers of the lutist picked out a tune. A simple tune, to be sure, but so haunting, so sad I hear it still, a song they called Deep Sorrow."

The old man closed his eyes. The café was quiet, with only a low murmur of voices and the occasional tinkling of silver. "I hear it still, as if I'd known it all my life, and lost it, and found it again, only to lose it once more."

Picard stared at the lowered eyelids of the old man, and listened for the haunting melody, hearing nothing but feeling it nonetheless, a tiny tune played along the nerves, as memories that weren't his own assailed his heart, filling him with the sense that he'd known it all before, that he'd been upon this case a hundred, a thousand times, that he'd tracked Lazare down through the ages, from one land and time to another, pursuing him ever and endlessly, accompanied by a tune, a haunting tune.

The old man hummed it softly, his eyes still closed, his gnarled fingers tapping the time lightly on the tabletop, the tune like the simple music of a carousel. Picard felt suddenly and hopelessly lost, upon a wooden horse which could never overtake the golden coach ahead of it on the wheel. Inside the fairy coach, Ric and Renée Lazare, forever free, mocked and laughed at him, as he spurred his wooden horse in pursuit of them.

"Enchantment, sir," said the old man, "the enchantment of the toys," His eyes, weak and watery, had covered with a thin film of tears, like a man submerged in a fishbowl, peering out through the glass, and Picard felt similarly immersed, in an ocean of anxiety, but he was determined to find the shore, to learn the secret of Lazare's past, to know and to win at last.

"This brilliant apprentice you speak of—how was he the cause of Robert Heron's sorrow?"

"The lad was possessed by a desire to be rich. He wanted to be a sort of monarch, covered in wealth. Heron and I argued with him, and Heron tried to make him understand that in the practice of the art one had to transcend the desire for riches, for that desire would find its way into the toys, and cause imperfections. Heron died virtually penniless, you know, with only a pauper to tend his grave. His reward, as he often said, was in the realm of the toys, where he was a king. But his disciple wanted to be a king of this world."

"A King of Paris, perhaps?"

"You've seen him?"

"It's possible."

"We lost sight of him before the fair was over. He'd grown impatient with our vow of poverty. And he'd already spied out the deepest part of Heron's work. *He's a master*, said Heron on the night we packed our tents in Buda. *God help him.*"

"Was there ever a fortune-telling machine?"

"According to Heron, all earthly events have their invisible beginnings. Through the toys one touched these unseen elements of nature and discerned the peculiar design of men's lives. Through the toys one could know the future, yes."

"That would be a formidable power."

"Robert Heron was a simple man, sir, and sought no such power. It was at his disposal but he did not use it."

"And his apprentice?"

"*He comes from Deep Sorrow*, Heron used to say. *He will return to Deep Sorrow*. And he'd wind the little lute player and listen to the song he'd made with his disciple, which haunted him to his grave, and will haunt me to mine."

Picard reached into the deep pocket of his Norfolk,

and brought out the acrobat he'd taken from Robert Heron's house. "Is this the apprentice?"

The pauper looked at the toy in wonder, his bushy grey eyebrows lifting high, as he nodded his head slowly up and down.

T H E train rumbled through the night, and Picard, seated alone in the dining car, placed the acrobat on the table and wound him up. The tiny replica of Ric Lazare performed faultlessly on the tablecloth; the night landscape sped by, firefly villages lost in an instant, replaced by somber forest. So Ric Lazare is no fool; of course I knew that. But he is also a craftsman, and craftsmen are the calmest of men, and the most cunning.

That shoemaker in Montmartre, the one I can never sneak up on, who greets me by name when I walk in the shop, though his back is always to the door. *But how do you do it, Monsieur Voutour? The shoes, Inspector, everyone's shoes have a different squeak.*

The craftsman, always a dangerous opponent.

Picard brought his thumb and forefinger together and letting his finger fly forward, knocked the little acrobat on the head. It fell over on its back, but a last turn of the idle spring must have been touched; the acrobat's knees came up, he flipped over and righted himself, standing once again before Picard's eyes.

He put the acrobat back into his pocket. Lights had appeared in the dark forest, solitary jewels followed now by shining clusters. Slowly the clusters grew larger until finally a great webbed necklace hung upon the night. Buda had meant many things to him in the past, but tonight it reminded him of the jewels around the neck of the little German princess the Baron had been escorting; and when I took aim the Baron's waistcoat seemed to be pressed against the muzzle of my pistol.

Picard walked slowly from the dining car, bending to peer out at the glittering Eastern Railway Station, the train pulling into the very center of the dazzling necklace, more brilliant and beautiful than he'd remembered it, as if enchanted by hidden spirits, or perhaps by the spirit of the brandy he'd been consuming in the dining car. But his heart was always gladdened by big cities, and he knew that in this he and Ric Lazare were similar. We both have a taste for glamor. Impossible to know how such tastes affect the aim. Certainly Lazare seems more ornate and in that way more encumbered, though you cannot consider Renée Lazare an encumbrance. Or if she is, let me be so encumbered, thought Picard, hauling down his valise from the storage rack.

❧

He slept well, had a dream, a wonderful one, of sitting beneath a tree and falling asleep there. This sleep-within-sleep produced a deep sense of well-being, so deep that for the brief moment of the dream he felt like a child again, wholly innocent and wise. At dawn he woke and went to the window of his hotel. It was on the bank of the Danube, facing the Royal Palace. The first rays of sun were now on the water, and barges were already moving through the clear morning. He dressed, and was strapping shut his bag when a servant of the hotel knocked on the door.

"If Monsieur is going to depart on the steamer . . ."

"Yes, thank you."

He settled his bill at the front desk, and walked into the street, taking the slow descent to the water's edge. The cries of the circling gulls echoed over the water and the smell of the river came to him. The pier he sought was enclosed by a wooden gate, and the ticket booth was just beyond it.

"Destination?"

"Esztergom."

He entered the pier and walked along it toward the gangplank. A smell of fish was in the air, and wet rope, and waterlogged wood. He climbed the gangplank and set his bag on deck, watching the other passengers come on board; no beautiful women at this hour of the morning. They're all still in bed, preserving their beauty.

The horn sounded and the lines were cast off. The gulls rose crying and wheeling with the captain as he steered away from shore. Picard walked along the ship's railing, until he was facing upriver into the wind. Somewhere in these hills, Ric Lazare was born, in the hidden valley called Deep Sorrow. He'd no doubt pay a fortune to eradicate that bit of information from his past.

Picard smiled toward the shoreline. The wise keep themselves invisible. But passports, visas, they trip a man up. Prince Solonski attempted to beat the game, traveling only with other people's luggage, had twenty-five passports, all with different names. One shuffles the deck . . .

He entered the lounge, where he ordered breakfast and studied a map of the region. Deep Sorrow—so insignificant as to have received no place on the map. But the hotel man thought . . . around here . . .

"Your coffee, sir."

Just beyond Esztergom. These hills and valleys change their name with each generation. But in here . . . a desolate area . . . well, I'll soon know.

He closed the map and opened the memoirs of Celeste Savidant. The shoreline slipped past and Mademoiselle Savidant slowly wrecked the life of the Duc de Rouleau, was receiving her next unsuspecting suitor as the steamer edged toward the dock at Esztergom. The local gulls swooped overhead, leading the ship with silent determination to her berth. Picard descended the gangplank, and went by carriage to number 14 Bajcsy Szilinszky Ut, the Bath Hotel, adjoined to a hot-spring spa. He entered the healing waters immediately after unpacking, and the numerous fatigues of traveling were slowly soothed. He soaked contentedly, and completed the reading of Mademoiselle Savidant's memoirs; the last beaten prince crawled penniless from her door and Picard stepped out of the steaming bath, leaving the book behind. Some other bather might come upon it and learn a valuable lesson; but one never learns. Celeste Savidant would swallow me up in an instant and I would be like all the rest, crawling broken from her doorstep. I know her building, on the chausée d'Antin. All very amusing, yes, until the victim is oneself.

"It's a wilderness," said the driver of the carriage. "And filled with thieves."

"Don't worry about thieves." Picard opened his jacket and laid his revolver on the seat beside him.

"Very well, we go."

The carriage was small, light, and the two horses that pulled it were fast. But the road soon became a miserable rutted affair, winding tortuously through the wooded hills. Picard sat directly behind the driver, in the open box, his cape wrapped close around him against the cold. The driver looked over his shoulder. "I know of only one family who lives in here."

"Then it is they whom we'll see."

"There were once many more families." The driver waved his arm toward the gloomy forest, then pointed to a space in the trees, where a road had once been, but where alder bushes grew now, blocking the way. "All abandoned. The life was too hard. Wolves, thieving gypsies, many things."

"And who is it that stayed?"

"A family of idiots."

Picard watched the bare forest pass. Snow had not yet fallen, but the wind and sky seemed to promise that it soon would. In a few weeks the road would be impassable, for no team of men would venture back to clear it. I've come in time, if there is anything to be found in this sorrowful valley.

The driver wheeled his carriage into a side road, which was obviously still being used, though it was hedged in close by poplars and other small trees. At the end of the road a crude peasant shack appeared, overflowing with children and ruled by an ape-like father, who stepped defiantly from the porch with an ax in his hand.

Picard stared toward the man, who stood perfectly still, as if made of Hungarian pig iron. The look in his eyes was related to a time before language, and the ax in his hand had the semblance of a club about it, so much so that Picard felt himself to be in a museum.

He knew what he must appear like himself, an aristocratic lord come to pick the pockets of the poor. Such has always been the case, and such it is now, thought Picard as he descended from the carriage, for I've come to pick your mind, if you have one.

The master of the hut didn't move, his expression seeming to reflect only a wish that he had brought another club from the closet of his shack, in order to have something in his left hand as well as his right. That not being possible, he slowly raised his left fist and held it silently in the air.

Picard twirled the late Baron Mantes's pistol-cane. I would not hesitate to fire it in your face, he said to the eyes of the ape-browed peasant.

The peasant's eyes followed the twirling cane closely, and his fingers opened and shut on his ax handle.

Picard carefully removed several large Hungarian bank notes from his pocket and flashed them in the peasant's face, naming the game.

The peasant's eyes underwent no transformation. Yes, thought Picard, I understand. Printed papers of any sort are not suitable to put in a pie. But even so . . .

The peasant turned his head slightly and grunted toward his shack. A woman came out wrapped in what appeared to be a pig's tablecloth, through which her large teats were manifesting angrily.

Picard spread the bills in his hand, holding them toward her. Yes, she has an instinctive understanding about money, perceives clearly that I'm offering the royal issue and not some bandit's bullshit.

He called to his driver. "Come here, and talk to this woman."

The driver came forward; Picard took the toy acrobat from his pocket and wound it up. The acrobat sprang from his hand, into the woman's astonished palm, where it landed and kicked again, to the ground. She cried out and her husband squatted down in amazement, astounded by the leaping toy, whose perfect somersaults on the dried grass looked like the movements of a lawn goblin, a creature he'd obviously long been looking for. He hesitated, therefore, to touch the creature, who went on bounding around in the trash of the front yard, his spring carrying him to the edge of a broken eggshell before it wound down, his tiny arm freezing and pointing to the cracked shell, as if trying to reveal something to those gathered on the lawn.

"Ask her if she knows who made that," said Picard, pointing to the toy.

The driver spoke to the woman slowly and gently, and she answered him, a satisfied smile on her face. The driver turned to Picard. "She says that she does, but she can't tell you his name, because he's a gypsy magician who would put the evil eye on her."

"Of course," said Picard, handing her one of the bank notes.

"Zoltán Lajos," said the woman, receiving the money. Her husband was flat on the ground, staring into the face of the acrobat. His children were seated around him, with less fear of the little creature. They knew it for the toy it was, and the oldest boy took the acrobat in his hands and wound it again.

"Ask her where Zoltán Lajos is from."

The driver spoke to the woman and she shook her head. Picard crossed her palm once more and she began talking in a guttural, nearly primeval dialect, the driver translating.

"Zoltán Lajos is from Dog Slope Mountain. She's seen him in the town of Dunabogdany. This was many years ago when she was young and beautiful."

"*A* toy like this," said Picard, to the hotel clerk in Dunabogdany. "Very detailed, complicated workings. Made
by a man called Zoltán Lajos."

The hotel clerk examined the piece for a moment, then
handed it back. "Our Mother of Holiness Church. They
have such a piece there. They wind it and play it for
weddings. It's supposed to bring the couple good luck."

"And does it?"

"I was married there and my wife left me for a fiddler."
The clerk smiled. "Good luck for me, yes. Bad luck for
the fiddler."

"This church . . ."

"Just beyond the square." The hotel clerk pointed, and
Picard left the hotel, crossed the square and entered the
church. It was quiet, nearly deserted. He walked up the
aisle, past a few kneeling women in black, and entered the
south vestibule. It contained only the usual announce-

ments, some folding chairs, a small painting of the risen Christ. Picard crossed in front of the altar and entered the north vestibule, which held several glass cases filled with objects of importance in the historical life of the parish—antique vestments, a piece of timber from the original and now vanished church which the present one had replaced, an elaborate music box on which two dancers stood, their arms around each other. They were dressed in the costume of bride and groom and the handiwork in the figures was that of Robert Heron, or a close disciple. Picard exited by the vestibule door and crossed the stone walk toward the parish house, a sleepwalker's air around him again, for he knew little of churches and their ways. The café was his church, and good food his communion.

❧

"What is your interest in Zoltán?"

"I'm from the Paris police," said Picard, showing his identification to the abbot.

The abbot nodded his head. "He made wonderful toys for the children, for the whole community. He was much loved when he lived here, for he had a gifted and generous nature. But his heart was angry. It caused his undoing."

"In what way?"

"He quarreled with a man, a local gambler. They fought. Zoltán stabbed him, the man died."

"Was Lajos imprisoned?"

"Certainly."

"In the state prison at Vác?"

"That is correct."

"Was he born in this region, Father?"

"He came to our town with the gypsies many years ago."

"He doesn't look like a gypsy."

"No, he does not. But then, he never said he was. He said . . ." The abbot hesitated.

"Yes, Father?"

"He said he was Egyptian."

"I'm told he possessed the evil eye."

"His greatest evil was his temper. It brought ruin to his soul."

"But what of this power he is supposed to have, to bring harm to others at a distance, by manipulating—the forces of nature."

"If he had such powers why did he stab Anton Romani in a public tavern?"

"Thank you for your help, Father," said Picard, standing.

The abbot rang his bell and the housekeeper came to show Picard out, down the long hallway of the parish house. His eyes were drawn to the painted dome of the entranceway—a pastel fresco to which age had given a luminous patina. Angelic spectators looked down at him from the rim of the inverted bowl, and Picard could not help smiling. It looked for all the world like a great crystal ball. In the center of it floated a pair of crossed golden keys, like signposts toward heaven. He pushed out through the door. He too possessed a key now, the master key needed to turn the lock on Ric Lazare. The toast of Paris had made the unfortunate mistake of killing a man in the open, with witnesses enough to convict him.

The warden of the state prison gestured toward Picard with his cigar. "Lajos was a born acrobat, climbed the side of our building like a fly." The warden pointed out the window to the high stone walls. In the distance, beyond the walls, the triumphal arch of Empress Maria Theresa commanded the skyline. Picard stared at her for a moment, feeling his own triumph nearing.

"I knew he'd scale the wall some day," said the warden. "We all knew it. We'd seen him demonstrate acrobatics to the other prisoners." The warden relit his cigar. "An ideal prisoner in many ways, I hope you can bring him back. Taught wood carving to the men. He seemed to enjoy prison life. Told me once that it was good to spend a certain amount of time in solitary confinement. Here's the full dossier on him."

Picard went through it quickly: Zoltán Lajos convicted of the murder of Anton Romani. Weapon an ice pick, during a quarrel over some dice Lajos had entered the game with. Romani lost the game, with an ice pick driven through the center of his forehead. Because Romani was an ex-convict, the death penalty was not brought. The warden received the dossier back. "You've got Lajos pinned?"

"I'll have him here inside a month."

"He's a slippery devil. Be on your guard."

"I'll bring him, but will your prison hold him?"

"More suitable arrangements can be made." The warden rose, showing Picard toward the door. "Stop in Debrecen, Inspector. The police there have had dealings with your man."

The inn beside the railway station was small, but held
a stage in back, roofed over by carefully tended vines,
beneath which a gypsy ensemble played. The goulash
was served with sweet fritters and gherkins, and the wine
was tokay, "the wine of kings, monsieur," said the waiter,
pouring for Picard.

"Enough," said Picard, holding up his hand. The small
bottle was three-quarters gone, and the waiter seemed
eager that he should finish it and begin another.

The gypsies played softly and Picard ate slowly; each
table was lit by a candle concealed inside deep-blue glass;
the candle flames quivered as the inn door opened and the
wind rushed in, accompanying a young woman. She was
dressed in a long sand-colored cape, had a proud and
independent air—releasing her cape into the waiter's outstretched hands and then following him to a table not
far from Picard. And she too was brought the wine of
kings.

Her presence caused a notable flurry among the gypsy
musicians, whose playing became instantly more seductive.
At the same time, their music continued to influence
Picard's elbow, as he pressed on with the kingly wine,
watching the woman all the while. Artificial violets were
entwined round her large purple hat, but there was nothing artificial about the expanse of soft flesh that showed
above the neckline of her jacket. Picard rose from his table
and walked into the back garden of the inn, where he
returned a portion of the wine of kings to the soil, taking
a breath of air and collecting his senses. The train does
not leave until morning. There's time for a dance.

He paused at the edge of the little vine-covered stage
and passed a bank note to the gypsy cymbolom player,

who received it with a knowing smile. Of course we will play a tune of enchantment, for that is our greatest pleasure. The fiddler stepped from the stage and made his way slowly round the room, followed by his associates.

The waiter stepped beside Picard. "We call it *mulnatni*, monsieur. Enjoying oneself with the gypsies."

Picard perceived that the woman's body was already moving, just faintly, in time to the fiddler's cunning song. She will spin her skirts tonight; her pretty legs will show.

The fiddler had begun an almost obscene display of musical ornamentation as he approached with his men to the woman's table. Grace notes, trills and flourishes filled the air and the guitar player began to sing.

"What is he saying?" asked Picard.

The waiter paused a moment to open another noble bottle, pouring for himself and Picard. As their glasses touched he said quietly,

> "*. . . they taught to me, those gypsies three,*
> *when life is saddened and cold,*
> *how to dream or play, or puff it away,*
> *despising it threefold.*"

Picard accepted a cigar from the waiter and they puffed away together, the smoke making him dizzy and he not caring, smoking to ease his nervousness as he prepared himself for the advance. His mind blew away, his body followed, light as a candle flame burning in blue glass, flickering, dancing, bewitched by music, wine, and the woman's high-heeled boot. He kept his gaze upon it, saw it moving discreetly beneath the table as the music gradually enveloped her. Slowly he took in the whole of her body with his look and when he reached her eyes he found that she was looking back at him.

"*H*E was called Bruno Bari when he operated here," said the Debrecen Chief of Police. "I'm quite sure it's the same fellow. Had an outstanding salon, entertained our finest citizens, and peddled an elixir of eternal life."

"Elixir?"

"An interesting scheme. It separated the aged Count Stephan Magor from a number of old family diamonds. Will you join me in coffee? Help yourself to the cream . . . the recipe for immortality required that the Count be starved for sixteen days, then bled, then given some white drops, bled again, and starved for thirty more days. The old boy went into convulsions, his hair and teeth fell out, and in this state he surrendered a good deal of his private property to Bruno Bari."

"Did he achieve his immortal wish?"

"He wears false teeth and a wig, and suffers, I am told,

from a delusion that he will last another fifty years, after which he will need a few more of the white drops."

"There were no charges brought against Bari?"

"It was too sensitive a case for us to touch, because of the Count's political position. And after one other minor incident we lost sight of Bruno Bari altogether."

"What was the other incident?"

"Not the sort of thing you can jail a man for."

"How so?"

"Sándor Zetti is one of the great merchants of the Hortobagy. He owns tremendous farm acreage there. Bruno Bari had the good fortune to steal Zetti's wife."

The estate of Sándor Zetti consisted of vast grazing land on both sides of the Hortobagy River. The master of the estate was out with his men, herding the horses. Would the Inspector care to ride out and join him?

Picard mounted a spirited black horse with a single white star on his forehead. A stable boy led the way on a second horse, out onto the plain. The day was bright, and unseasonably warm. Picard enjoyed the sleek powerful body of the horse between his legs. His injured testicle performed its usual hide-and-seek game, creeping away from the horse's spine and taking refuge in the Inspector's abdomen. He felt it hiding, felt the painful tug in his guts. He pulled his stomach tight and concentrated on the horse's flowing mane, the bobbing head, the sound of the hooves.

In the distance, he saw the flying cloaks of the Hortobagy horsemen, and the dust from their racing mounts.

Ranks closed up and Picard was racing alongside the horsemen, whose whips were cracking over a herd of splendid horses.

The men's faces were dusty, weather-beaten, and their moves instinctively graceful. Picard matched them to the best of his abilities as they circled the herd, his cloak rising up as exuberantly if not as brightly as the loose purple capes of the horsemen. The air was filled with whipcracks and thundering hooves, and Picard rode joyously over the sprawling plain, in company with the men, lifting his cry with theirs, turning the horses with them.

When the herd was finally calmed and the dust had started to settle, a man as barrel-chested as Picard came riding up. He was obviously master of the estate, his eyes sweeping over it, and over Picard, with the look of a man used to having his way.

Picard held out his police shield. "I'm searching for Bruno Bari."

"When you find him, please inform me." They trotted side by side, while the other horsemen raced ahead.

"Tell me what you know about him."

"He stole my wife," said Master Zetti, tugging at his heavy mustache. "A whore, but what a whore, the most beautiful prostitute in Buda. You've seen her?"

"Yes," said Picard, seeing her instantly in his mind, her body moving through his memory, her breasts trembling in his brain.

Zetti smiled for the first time. "I see that you have met her." He laughed, patting his horse on the neck. "I was the highest bidder. Every man of wealth in Buda sought her favor. And what favor, what rare and priceless favor it was. I lost more than money when she left, though she took off with a great deal of that, as well. Of course, she had to have the best."

"Did Bruno Bari take any of your property?"

"He took my soul, which was not my property. Look, Inspector, look up there and tell me what you see."

Ahead in the sky was a herd of running horses, shimmering, fantastic, galloping through the blue dome of heaven.

Picard blinked his eyes, watched the horses racing off into the endless reaches of the sky.

"A mirage, Inspector. The fabulous Fata Morgana. Bruno Bari was fascinated by it, by which he showed himself to be a true peasant. Only the peasants let the mirage rule their life, daydreaming over it. He always talked about it, making it sound rare, philosophical. Like all the other famous liars around here, he claimed to have gone walking through the Fata Morgana, through paradise." Sándor Zetti spat on the ground and spurred his horse.

Picard touched his own mount with his heels and they raced toward the floating paradise in the sky, where the horses of heaven roamed, but he and Zetti came no closer. Earth-bound, they were unable to rise up and run with the celestial herd, and their galloping slowed again to a trot.

"Some days you'll see entire forests floating in the air. Lakes and valleys and hills, all golden, with perhaps a cow sailing over the whole of it." Zetti turned to Picard. His eyes were suddenly questioning, and in the question was a small boy, in pain. "Have you seen Renée with Bari?"

"He's called Ric Lazare now. They're in Paris."

"Yes, she loved the high life. And how is she looking? Don't tell me, or we shall both appear ridiculous." Zetti spurred his horse once more and the two men rode across the last part of the field, bringing their horses to the stable, where the grooms received them. "I chased him myself, unsuccessfully." They walked from the stables toward the house. "You saw my men, Inspector. Relentless riders. We tore this half of Europe apart trying to catch Renée and Bari, but we could not, though we saw them twice. They vanished, like the Fata Morgana. You'll dine with me, of course."

The dining room of the mansion was built around a huge stone fireplace. The windows were of stained glass, which gave an iridescent quality to the sunlight as it filtered through onto the long massive wooden table, the tabletop aglow with quiet light, the soup tureen and serving plates part of a fabulous Fata Morgana—beautiful, delicately tinged, through which the hand passed, never quite able to grasp the streaming color. Picard reached for bread, and turned golden; leaned back through a band of blue, and settled in a pool of red light which surrounded his chair, a wanderer come to the rainbow's end and served with fairy food in a gossamer room. The voice of his host brought him back from his daydream, but even so, Zetti's face was bathed in gold, like some titan of the rainbow, ferocious and chimerical, and Picard could not escape the peculiar feeling that his chase was leading him still deeper into mirage, into a danger more subtle than any he'd ever faced in the brutal Parisian underworld.

"He came here as her guest. Quite often." Zetti sipped his wine. "Renée loved his toys. He had a wonderful gift that way, I must admit. It fascinated Renée, and charmed me, and while I was so charmed, they stole off together."

"You say you followed them?"

"Into the mountains of Transylvania. Fifteen men surrounded the inn in which we'd cornered them. But he slipped by us, heaven knows how. We picked up his trail again at the base of the Mountain of Skulls. There is a ruined castle there. As we made our way up the mountainside, one of my men suddenly clutched at his chest and fell to the ground, as if he'd been struck by—by a poisoned dart. He muttered hysterically that Bruno Bari was a sorcerer, and by the time we got the man under shelter he was dead, without a mark on his body. He was a young man, in perfect health. I abandoned the chase at that point, in regard for my men."

"That was the end of your knowledge of Bari?"

"There was a newspaper account of the death of a young priest, in the convent gardens of the Metropolitan of Transylvania. The priest had recently been involved in an argument with a traveling magician, or charlatan, call him what you will. I know it was Bruno Bari, and I call him a filthy dog."

"In what manner did the priest die?"

"The coroner's report was apoplexy. This was, by the way, the same diagnosis given of my man who died upon the Mountain of Skulls."

*I*N the wild and sinister mountains of Transylvania, Picard felt again the strange vertigo he'd known in Austria. He should, by rights, be heading now toward Paris. His case was complete. And yet there was a nerve end that thrilled toward this death by apoplexy of a young Transylvania priest. And so he continued on by carriage, through winding and inhospitable terrain. Something said he must go on past the mountaintop castles and through the rugged villages where the peasants sat in their doorways, smoking long black pipes. The doors and window frames were intricately carved in mystical whorls, depicting the soul of a highly imaginative and somewhat fantastic people.

It was with relief that he reached the city of Bucharest, finding it wholly normal and bourgeois, untouched by the morbid quality of the peasant art which had worked upon his spirit for so many lonely miles. The hotel sent his message to the Metropolitan of Transylvania, who responded at once. His Holiness would see the Inspector at two in the afternoon.

Picard arrived punctually at the palace gates. He was admitted into a large park. Tame deer strolled through an avenue of trees, and in front of the holy palace a fabulous procession of peacocks was passing.

He was shown down a long stone hallway to the receiving room of the Metropolitan, an elderly man in long soutane and crowned by a high red calette.

"Your Grace." Picard bowed to the old priest.

The Metropolitan summoned his footman and jam was served in little glass plates. The two men touched at the spread with small silver spoons. "Whatever you can tell me about the death of Father Miklós, and of the magician with whom he quarreled . . ."

"Father Miklós and I were walking together, on the palace grounds. It was a quiet, beautiful day. Suddenly the deer, who had been feeding close by us, ran away terrified, as if they'd caught scent of something in the wind. The peacocks screeched wildly. Father Miklós turned to me, with a deep sadness in his eyes. He sank to the grass, dead at my feet."

"Dead of apoplexy."

"That is correct," said the old priest. "Of course, the servants and the local people made much of the terror of the birds and deer. And they inevitably linked it to Father Miklós having had a run-in with a traveling mesmerist, whom he ordered out of the city on the previous day." The Metropolitan paused, tapping his small silver spoon upon his front teeth. "Our people are very superstitious. It is not good to stir them up with such things as this mesmerist was reputed to have been performing."

"Such as?"

"Oh, telling fortunes, and causing people to act in strange ways against their will. Suggestiveness is very deeply seated in the human heart, I'm afraid," said the Metropolitan. "So we took steps against the man. His name was . . ." The old priest paused again. "I think it was the Great Baltus, a name of that sort anyway, the usual pompousness these people have. Father Miklós visited him, and by a coincidence met his death not twenty-four hours later."

"You see no connection?"

"I have lived a good many years, Inspector, and have seen many strange and terrible things. But without exception, their origin was in accord with the accepted laws of causality. I am not trying to make less of a tragic death. Father Miklós was like a son to me. But his passing was not mysterious, only unfortunate for being premature. As to the animals, I'm sure you are aware how sensitive animals are to impending death."

"Did you see this mesmerist?"

"He was described as a lean man, with a metallic brightness in his eyes, of the kind one sees in the eyes of an epileptic. His wife was said to be of special beauty. There are many such gypsies traveling the roads. They are no different from the rest of mankind."

Picard rose. "I'm grateful for your time, Excellency."

"Please," said the old priest, "take this." He reached into his soutane and withdrew an embroidered piece of cloth, hung on a thin red string. Upon it was woven the descent of a white dove.

Picard slipped the amulet into his pocket, and bowed again to the old priest. The footman showed him down the hallway and out of the palace. On the grounds were the tame deer who had bolted at the premonition of Father Miklós's death. They were nibbling quietly now, undisturbed by such intuitions.

S N O W was falling in Paris; he stood on the Pont-Neuf and stared upriver, his bag beside him on the walk. The towers and bridges were wrapped in the storm, but the snow didn't stick, was melting on the ground, on his outstretched hand, and he melted into the familiar façades, feeling it all again, Paris, a trap, a sewer. Nonetheless, I'm happiest in you. I've been visiting your sisters, and they can't compare with you. You're my one madness, and I know you'll ruin me in the end. But I'm glad to be here.

He picked up his bag, crossed the rest of the way over the river, and entered the Latin Quarter. The voices of the street, the smells coming from the café kitchens, the familiar swirl of life on the rue Dauphine were as soothing as the healing waters in far-off Esztergom. I'll open my rooms first, let some air in, change my clothes—and there are the lovely lemon tarts. Pass, Picard, pass and keep your belt hooked tight.

The rue de Nesle was mean-looking and squalid as ever, and he walked along it happily to the battered doorway of his tenement. The concierge looked up from his den, where he was stroking a cat, and gave a sleepy-eyed, half-drunken nod. He hasn't noticed I've been gone. A building like this is one in a million.

Picard climbed the stairs to the fifth floor, which he shared with Saulnier. The degenerate philosopher's door was open and a rotten smell filled the hallway. "Hey, Saulnier, what are you cooking in there, a dead rat?"

Saulnier came out of the gloomy depths of his rooms, and squinted at Picard through thick glasses. "I smelled it myself, about a quarter of an hour ago." He stroked his tangled beard and twitched his nose. "I think it's in your place."

Picard looked toward his door, saw the faint curl of smoke from beneath it. He fumbled with his key, threw open the door and raced into the stinking smoke, into a nightmare repeated, a burning room, suffocating hands at his throat. He lost his momentum, swayed in the smoke, confusion gripping him. A shadow moved, he raised his arm to guard against the Baron's descending cane.

"Water!" called Saulnier, stumbling past him.

Picard staggered to the window, drew it open. The wind sucked the nauseating smoke into the street, and

Picard turned, saw the smoldering black lump which had almost burned out now, in the ashtray on the living-room table. And of course there was no Baron, the Baron is dead and under the ground in Nuremberg. But I saw him, saw him coming at me just now. Into your grave, Mantes, our fight is done.

Saulnier came from the kitchen with a glass of wine in his hand. "There is no water."

"It's out," said Picard, pointing at the offensive black lump.

"Then I shall drink the wine."

Picard went to the table and looked at the lump, from which a last foul fume was rising. "Did you see anyone in the hall?"

Saulnier set the wine glass down. "It was probably Josie's kid, the little bastard. Last month he hung a dead fish behind my bed."

Picard went to the kitchen and found the window latch open. "He came through here." The crude fire escape was empty, as was the courtyard below.

"I smelled it all month in my room, Picard. A sickly-sweet odor. I tore the place apart. Then—behind my bed, hanging on a string, a dead mackerel."

Picard returned to the living room, and touched the lump with the tip of his pocketknife. A tongue of foul blackness bubbled out of the incision, dissolving into an oily stream that ran along his blade. "This was not done by a child."

"He has a viciously twisted mind, Picard. You don't know the boy the way I do."

Picard took out his handkerchief and laid it over the warm lump, wrapping it up carefully.

Saulnier went to the kitchen window and looked down into the courtyard. "He's probably in the cellar some-where, enjoying a laugh. I practically lost my sanity over that fish. Unable to find the origin of the smell, I had begun to believe that I was the cause of it, that I was in some way undergoing a strange putrefaction." Saulnier returned to the living room. "When I finally found it, it was so rotten it had entered a state of phosphorescence. It glowed in the dark, Picard, that kid's fish. I flung it into the alley. That night the cats went berserk. You should have heard them screaming."

<hr />

Picard walked the pale yellow hall toward the Prefect's office, and removed his storm-soaked cloak at the door. The snow had turned to rain, and it beat upon the win-dows now, as he knocked on the Prefect's door and entered.

"Inspector," said the Prefect's assistant, rising from his desk and extending his hand. "Good to see you back. Nice work with Mantes. The Chief was very pleased."

"Is he in?"

"He won't be back until five."

"Did you receive papers of extradition from the Hun-garian police?"

"The Lazare case, yes," said the assistant, returning to his desk. "The Prefect wants to speak with you about that."

"Lazare hasn't left Paris, has he?"

"He seems in no hurry to leave. I understand his wife has inaugurated the practice of bathing in champagne."

Picard sat on a favorite bench on the Champs-Elysée, rubbing his hands nervously, staring at the little birds beyond him, who pecked in the pebbles for pieces of bread. The storm had passed, and the sun was attempting to break through. The four o'clock bells chimed. An hour to go. But the Prefect is always punctual. We'll have Lazare under arrest by six.

He rose and walked on through the park, to a large round pool surrounded by rusty metal chairs. Now the clouds were completely vanquished by the sun; he sat and stared at its reflection in the filthy water. Imprisoned carp circled beneath the surface, and the sun played on their muddy scales, their sores, their gaping mouths, as they nosed at bits of trash that floated above them. Those men who hated him most were all in prison—Alexandre Syrette, Gaston Perèse, Maurice de Merchant—making their afternoon rounds at this moment, biting at old cigar butts in the prison yard. And you'll soon join them, Lazare. You can teach them wood carving.

He rose again, unable to remain in one spot, the final nervousness of the hunt upon him now. The next long pathway took him through the trees once more, toward the next glittering pool in the distance. The snow of the morning had melted everywhere, the trees and lawns were bare, but the wind continued and as he neared the pool he saw the tiny sailboats moving there.

It was a favorite spot, and he often rented one of the

crude little sailboats which a peddler provided for idle enthusiasts of the sport. The peddler was there today and Picard walked toward his cart.

"Yes, monsieur, here's a fine red one . . . she'll take the wind for you . . ."

Picard launched the red boat, and it joined the many others which were going amongst the carp, who circled like whales beneath the little ships. Most of the boats were like his—a roughly hewn hull, a single sail. But occasionally he'd seen exceptional craft on these waters, built by old sailors with time on their hands and loving memories to guide them. One such ship was sailing today— a Spanish galleon, its many sails filling with the wind. His own boat had been driven back against the wall of the pool, and he let it float there, going with the crowd toward the galleon that was now sailing obediently toward its owner. They gathered around him, Picard amongst them. A slender polished cane was extended toward the Spanish vessel, and the owner's arm came forward.

Picard moved his hand toward his revolver.

"Inspector," said Ric Lazare, touching the boat with his cane and thrusting the little craft back into the wind. Beside him knelt Renée, in an old-rose gown. Both she and Lazare were calmly watching the water, as unruffled as a pair of Parisian pigeons, while Picard stood embarrassed, slowly lowering his hand from within his jacket.

"And how is your investigation proceeding, Inspector?" Lazare got to his feet and examined the tip of his cane. "I understand you've been traveling—on the trail of a rogue."

Picard turned to Renée Lazare. "I trust you continue to enjoy our city, madame."

Renée smiled at Picard. "Oh yes, so many fascinating people. You must come to our salon again, Inspector."

"But of course," said Picard, glancing back toward Lazare, who seemed lost in contemplation, his eyes having once again taken on their strange and metallic lustre, as if he had learned to command the very edge of a seizure, a fine and fearful edge.

"If you have left anything unfinished in your life," said Lazare, "I suggest you attend to it. Because tomorrow you die."

I could kill him now, break his arrogant neck. But there's no need of that. Control yourself, Picard. In an hour, he's yours. "My only unfinished business is you, monsieur. I shall do my best to swiftly complete it."

"You think you'll take me so easily?" Lazare extended his cane once more toward the galleon, which was again approaching in the wind.

"I'll take you," said Picard softly.

Lazare touched the beautiful ship, this time bringing it to the edge of the pool and removing it from the water. "How deeply you deceive yourself, Inspector. Have you no understanding?" Lazare wiped the brightly polished decks with his handkerchief, and the jeweled silver ring on his index finger caught Picard's eye. Within the perfect gem a figure seemed to move, no bigger than a hair, but there, unmistakably so—a tiny man walking through a crystalline garden. The ring flashed as Lazare turned his hand, and the scene was gone, but Picard was left with the distinct feeling of himself being trapped in an icy and transparent wasteland. His heart shuddered violently and he forced his gaze toward the water, where a lazy carp broke the surface with his tail, then slipped out of sight.

"Good day, Inspector," said Lazare cheerfully, putting the little galleon under one arm and his ravishing wife on the other, as he turned and walked away.

THE five o'clock bells chimed. The Prefect stared at Picard for a moment, then resumed his shuffling of dossiers. "There's no way we can touch the man. I've already telegrammed to the Hungarian police, explaining it was a case of mistaken identity."

Picard looked at the floor; his head felt like marble, and his fine hunting edge was gone. "How did he . . . ?"

"He got to the Emperor, and made himself untouchable. You're aware, I'm sure, that Louis Napoleon is highly superstitious."

"I've heard it."

"Well, Lazare has favorably impressed him, with predictions and such. Louis now fancies Lazare as some sort of court magician. Thus it is impossible for us to arrest him."

"A murderer."

"He will not be the first murderer to advise a king." The Prefect swiveled in his chair, turning toward the river. Evening had settled on the city; a few raindrops again touched the windows. "There's a costume ball tonight, given by Count Cherubini for the Great Whores of our city. He's requested police protection. Would you care to attend?"

"Very well."

"It might prove amusing. Nonetheless, keep a close watch. La Païva will be there, wearing her jewels."

"I shall do my best."

"Yes, and keep an eye on the Count too. After his last affair we found him on the embankment, riding a perfumed donkey. He was accompanied by a woman clad only in lilacs."

"I'll watch him until sunrise."

"Good. The assistant has your invitation. Pick it up from him on the way out."

Picard turned to go, was stopped by the Prefect's low musing voice: "Whores and magicians, Picard, that is Paris now. Do you believe in fortunes?"

Picard remained silent, and the Prefect looked up at him. "Yes, it's all nonsense, isn't it. Do you know that a horoscope was cast at Louis's birth? It indicated he would become Emperor of France."

Picard left the Prefect, walked the halls of the great complex like one in a dream. Lazare has succeeded, he'll be a Prince of Paris now.

. . . *Because tomorrow you die.*

I wonder, Lazare, are you one of those who play the

game for the highest stakes? For if you are—if you're like David Orléans, who resented the least little salt on his tail—then perhaps you do mean to murder me.

In which case I must make certain arrangements of my own. For there is another law, Lazare, a law higher even than the Emperor's law.

The law of the jungle, monsieur. Perhaps you've heard of it in your vast travels.

Picard entered the laboratory wing of the Prefecture, and walked down the windowless corridor. Of course, it could all be bluff, for Lazare is filled with that too. Difficult to know what is true and what is false with one so pompous. There is, however, the ice pick in the head. That was decidedly real for the man who dared to suggest that Lazare's dice were not quite correct.

"Hello, Renan, do you have anything for me?"

The head of the laboratory looked up from his test tubes and microscopes. "I've analyzed it," he said, pointing to the stinking black lump which sat at the far edge of his bench, in a metal box. "A rather peculiar concoction."

"It smelled like hell when it was burning."

"That was the sulphur and iron filings. It also contains gum ammoniac, and parts of a plant from the spurge family." The lab chief pushed his glasses back on his head and drew the black lump toward him. "However, the principal components are the blood of a man and the brain of an animal. Know any witches, Picard?"

"I'll take it off your hands," said Picard, wrapping the black lump in his handkerchief again. "Thanks, Renan."

"Anytime, Picard. I'm always interested in new combinations."

Picard closed the lab door behind him and went along the corridor toward the exit; he was already in the courtyard when he remembered the invitation to the whores' ball and turned, back toward the Prefect's office.

"The Chief said there was an invitation needed for the ball tonight."

"I sent it down to your desk."

He entered the adjacent office, from which he and the other inspectors operated. It was empty now, as it almost always was, for he and Veniot and Bazin rarely used the small oak desks appointed them. He went to his own, and picked up the invitation.

The side drawers were a jumble, filled with old papers and scraps of information on cases that were finished, as was the Lazare case now—a case for the scrap bin. He opened the center drawer, and noticed a crudely wrapped package he could not identify. He severed the black twine which bound it and laid open the paper around a bloody calf's heart, pierced through with thorns.

<hr />

The Seine murmured beneath the bridge. He stared at the water and followed the murmuring, trying to follow it to the sea, but the carriages and voices of the early evening obscured the dark passage; he could not slip away.

His pocket was heavy; he lightened it, dropping the bloody heart and the stinking black lump into the river. They made a small splash and were gone, to feed the eels.

He walked on, into the Quarter. The streets were already crowded with evening couples, and the little cafés and restaurants had begun to fill. Over it all was the vague sense of distortion which had troubled him for weeks, as if all these good solid Parisians were in danger of slipping away, of being devoured in the vast jaws of night, never to be seen again. Their lives, their laughter, their wines and meals were tenuous, fragile, like wisps of smoke upon a haunted street. The smiling girl in the window—a spectre, moving through a lost land.

How morbid Lazare has made me. But this is precisely what he does to those who visit his parlor—distorts their life, twists their imagination, makes them doubt everything but his word. But you cannot control all of us, Lazare. Some of us, the dullest perhaps, refuse to be deceived.

The broken door of his building admitted him, and the concierge waved from his room, knocking things about as he prepared for the night's card game. Picard smiled, returning the wave, glad for low life, rotten smells, twisted stairs. Your crystal ball, Monsieur Lazare, would mean nothing to the tenants here, for their reputations are without value, their fortunes already lost, their fate irreversible.

He climbed to his landing, walked down the creaking hall to his door. It would be pleasant to catch Lazare in my room and cut his throat directly.

But the apartment was empty, had not been entered again. The old leather armchair greeted him with its many smiling scars, and he sat down in it, opening his jacket and removing the tiny acrobat from his pocket.

The red thread of the Holy Ghost amulet had caught around the acrobat's neck. Picard looped the thread over the gas lamp, and the acrobat dangled there, casting a hanged man's shadow on the wall.

C o u n t Cherubini's courtyard was already filled with other carriages, from which men and women in extravagant costume were descending. Picard's costume was a black evening suit with the addition of a black satin mask, sewn with bits of sequin.

The entranceway was blazing with light, and butlers framed the doorway, admitting the gods and goddesses of fantasy. Picard climbed the staircase toward the door. The butler on the left accepted his invitation and the one on the right escorted him into the luxurious dwelling, taking him to the cloakroom, where his hat and cape were received.

"You're from the Prefecture? Count Cherubini will speak with you. Please follow me." Picard trailed the butler down the towering hallway. Upon the ceiling painted nymphs sported with goat-legged men bearing grapes. The Count was standing at the entranceway to the main ballroom, dressed as a rooster; he nodded his comb to Picard as the butler whispered that it was another of the Prefect's men.

"May I point out certain objects I'd like you to watch closely, Inspector?" The brightly feathered cock directed his beak toward Mademoiselle Tardivel, dressed as Juno, a brilliant necklace sparkling above her celebrated bosom. "Half a million francs," said the rooster softly.

Picard swept his eyes further along, to where the great cock winked: Mademoiselle Bourque as Aphrodite, jewels sewn in strategic places on her transparent costume. "Three hundred thousand francs," sighed the rooster. "Many of them mine. Well, then, enjoy yourself, Inspector. None but I know your identity."

The grand ballroom was lined with mirrors; the costumed figures seemed reflected down an endless hallway. Picard stared into its depths, finding himself among the other masqueraders, his mask of night repeated to infinity.

"Mademoiselle Chessie, as 'The Nymph' of Ingres, a living portrait."

He turned toward the door, where the butler's announcement had ushered in a completely naked young woman. The excited rooster was walking beside her, his comb quivering from side to side.

Picard made his way through horns, feathers, ribbons, swords, past a man bound from head to feet with butcher's twine. At the buffet table were two popes, eyeing each other's cassocks contemptuously. Picard took a plate of food and turned back toward the center of the room.

"Miss Carter, of America, as the Southern Belle."

The butler at the doorway stepped aside, admitting a

young lady, who entered the room in a hammock carried by two half-naked Negroes.

The room sparkled with jewelry and the mirrors echoed the glittering arms and throats and gesturing fingers. Picard sought out his colleagues, found Inspector Turcotte, who like himself wore a simple black mask.

"*Salud,*" said Turcotte, raising a champagne glass.

"Who else of us is here?"

"Lescadre is circulating upstairs at the moment," said Turcotte with a smile.

"Circulating?"

"Checking doors and windows. The maids are showing him around."

"We might not see him for a while."

"And when we do, his knees will be trembling." Turcotte placed his glass on the tray of the passing waiter, and took two more, handing one to Picard. "To the Count."

"To the Count." They clicked their glasses toward the dazzling rooster, who was attempting to climb into the hammock with Miss Carter.

"A wonderful man," said Turcotte. "You know his fortune is gone. This house is all that's left of it."

"If that were all that were left of my fortune . . ."

"But he started with millions. Lost it all on horses and whores. I understand he pimps for the Emperor now." Turcotte turned with his wine glass, lifting it toward a large portrait of Louis Napoleon that commanded the high central wall over the door. The Emperor looked out of the canvas with unblinking eye, staring over the sea of masqueraders, his gaze going deep into the realm of the mirrors, where he too was repeated, again and again, in an endless succession of Napoleons.

"Ernest Duval—'A Humble Priest.'"

The lean young confidence man entered the room, his monk's robe trailing on the floor. Music had begun, played by three men clad in brief togas, their heads wreathed in leaves, their fingers moving over double-reed pipes and a lyre. The Humble Priest, the star women, the goddesses, the birds of paradise, the rooster himself—all began to dance.

"Drink!" crowed the rooster to his guests. "Drink to drunkenness!"

Picard parted from Turcotte, went along the precipitous depths of the mirror, where gods and goddesses moved in their infinite dance. Again he saw himself in the enchanted glass, suddenly felt the secret of the labyrinth and sought to break through the mirror's soul, but it retreated, becoming more subtle and more dangerous, its feathers and its winking jewels calling him still deeper.

He turned from the dizzying embrace and exited from the ballroom, toward the kitchen. The servants were coming and going through the doorway, bearing trays laden with food and drink. The chef and his assistants were clad in white, working steadily, but lightheartedly, having obviously sampled much of the wine.

Picard approached one of the staff, a young man dreaming idly by a large coffee urn. "I'm from the Prefecture," said Picard. "Does this area give access to the courtyard?"

The young coffee brewer led him through the gesticulating ranks of the chefs, to an outer hall, and a locked door. "Are you expecting trouble?"

"One never knows," said Picard. "There's a lot of ice floating in the ballroom."

"The Great Whores," said the young man, opening the door. "I wonder if they're any better than the rest."

"Save your money and find out." Picard stepped into the rear courtyard.

It was long and narrow, and he went through it slowly, in the shadows. The windows were all high, and locked. He sat on a stone bench and watched for an hour, alone. No one came or went in the garden, except for the cats of St. Honoré, who prowled quietly along the walls and fences.

Bare trees whispered in the garden, creaking coldly, gently, and he watched for another hour, pacing slowly along the winding lanes of the yard. The arbor was dry, rattled in the wind; the busts of the Cherubini family stood in the garden, listening to the squandering of the ancestral fortune. Picard went along the side of the house, and entered the front courtyard once again.

The carriage men were standing together, talking, laughing, and the horses waited patiently, covered by rough blankets. He crossed the cobblestones, going toward the main door. The butlers, both slightly drunk, were flirting with the cloakroom maids and took no notice of him as he entered. He walked to the ballroom, found Turcotte and Lescadre, who were also beginning to sway in their tracks.

"They're giving it away," said Lescadre. "Upstairs in a solid-gold bathtub." He drained his champagne glass and reached for another. "The Great Whores are giving it away free tonight."

"Except for La Païva," said Turcotte, pointing with his glass. Picard saw a voluptuous creature, dressed as a strawberry ice, her body covered with jewels.

"You know the saying," continued Turcotte. "Nothing for free from La Païva. But she'll fuck a miner for a nugget."

Picard stared at the millionairess, who was dancing with a lizard.

"The lizard is a woman," said Lescadre. "I encountered her in the bath."

The lithe green lizard was held in the jeweled arms of the Queen of Whores, and they spun gracefully to the music. Picard followed them with his eyes as they danced past Duval, the Humble Priest, who was speaking to a toad. He had produced a business portfolio from within his robe, and the toad was peering into the workings of Eldorado Investments.

"Give me sixteen cups of wine!" crowed the rooster from the center of the room. "For I love drunkenness!"

The passing waiter stopped beside the inspectors. "Gentlemen, some refreshment?"

"Yes, thank you," said Turcotte, taking more champagne, and serving Picard and Lescadre. He turned toward the full-length portrait of the Empress which commanded the other side of the room, high over the south-central door.

"To the Empress."

"To Eugénie."

"Cheers."

Picard stared at the portrait of the beautiful Spaniard,

whose long red hair flowed down over her milk-white bosom. Turcotte laid his hand on Picard's shoulder. "Save your dreaming, she's a cold fish."

Lescadre reached for another glass of champagne. "I find that hard to believe."

Turcotte turned toward Louis's portrait. "The Emperor also found it hard to believe. He was expecting Spanish blood and got an icicle in his bed."

"She should try the Count's golden bathtub," said Lescadre. "Warm waters to relax her. Skilled hands to . . . what is it, Picard, what do you see?"

"If you gentlemen will excuse me . . ."

"Certainly. Enjoy yourself, Picard. Turcotte and I will protect the realm."

Picard moved through the dancers, drawn to a linen-clad, moon-masked girl. She might be ugly as a turkey; such are the chances one takes at costume balls, where certain half-blessed, half-cursed women take advantage of the night of masks.

He followed the linen-clad body, as she danced by with an ancient Roman statesman in a long toga. *His paunch is worse than mine; and he's lost his hair. When the music ends . . .*

He waited close by, following their dance. *It's the linen, the way her hips move within it, impossible to resist them. Therefore, noble senator . . .*

The music ceased. He stepped forward. "May I bring you some refreshment?"

The moon-mask turned toward him, the silver lips smiling.

The Roman senator arched his eyebrow, his bald head reflecting the light of the chandelier. "Am I to understand the next dance is taken?"

"You understand correctly," said Picard, taking the girl's hand and leading her among the fairy-tale couples who were again moving to the weird Pan-like music of the leaf-crowned musicians.

He tried to keep his bootheels off her sandaled feet. She met his body with her breasts, her thighs, her instep. He drew her closer against him, lowering his hand to her hip, resting it there, feeling its movement as she circled with him, the other dancers pressing them still closer together. Their movements had almost ceased, their bodies locked below the waist, she undulating against him, and he burning against her thigh. The mirror was just behind her; he stared over her shoulder, enjoying the shape of her backside, and letting himself reel out into the mirror's depths, now that he had a partner on the dazzling vertiginous glide toward infinity. They turned inside the glass, a thousand Picards, a thousand moon-maids, with thousands more beyond them, ever diminishing Picard and his soft moon-partner in the cavern of mirrors, the vertigo increasing until he could stand the mirror's madness no longer, its dazzling avenues somehow threatening, reminding him too much of Lazare and crystal balls, of an evil thousand-eyed sorcery that makes a man see depths which are not there, see avenues of light that are mere reflection, see people who don't exist.

He turned the moon-girl slowly, to the music, caught a glimpse of Louis's portrait, then the Empress's, reflected in the depths, and they too have been caught in Lazare's glass. He has the big fish in his bowl now, Picard. Can you doubt for a moment that he means to rub you out, now that he stands to gain so much, and you have threatened his game?

"Have you forgotten me?" asked the moon-girl softly, through her mask.

"The mirror—" He opened his hand toward it. "I followed you into it."

"Beware of mirrors, then," she said. "They make you forget what's real." She moved her thighs, so that her own warmest part came against his, its soft contours making a suggestion he took at once, dancing her toward the staircase.

There was but one piece of furniture in the tiny upstairs pleasure grotto—a soft velvet couch on which she lay. "Don't be so gentle," said the moon-maid, as he fumbled with her shoulder strap.

The walls of the room were papered in muted reds, and the couch was framed by two large crystal bowls in which small candles floated, illuminating her white mask, her clinging gown. Picard knelt beside her, his fingers finally succeeding with the strap. The cloth fell away from her breast. He bent his head and kissed the nipple, tasting oil of lilies on his tongue.

The moon-girl breathed heavily, her eyes closing within the dark craters of her mask. He unbuttoned the other linen band, rolling his face in the cleavage of her breasts as she pulled her thin dress down and slipped it off her ankles. He reached for her mask, lifting it from her face.

"Why do you draw back?" she asked, her eyes shining with the same unnatural brightness as her husband's. "You should enjoy yourself while you can." Madame Lazare smiled, unbuttoning the top button of his jacket. "Because tomorrow you die."

He stood, chilled, even as her magnificent body filled him with lust. To ride those thighs, to plunge into her curling black hair, to ravish her, to roll with her in insane abandon—he was pounding with desire for one devastating tumble with the angel of Paris—but some instinct of self-preservation held him back, for the look in her gleaming eyes was inhuman, the look of a devouring angel whom it would be death to love, who would carry him still deeper into the already powerful net of his enemy. And he touched her anyway, wanting to lose himself, risk the greater depths, go mad with her on the couch—and again he drew back, sensing an entanglement of arms and legs and glittering eyes from which he could never extricate himself. He stepped away, with the nightmarish sensation that he was already completely entangled, that there was no way to escape her. But that's every woman's game, Picard, wake up, you idiot, and get out of here before she puts a knife to your throat.

"You should kiss the amulet of renewal," she said, raising her hips toward him.

"I've kissed such amulets before."

"Mine is like no other."

"I see no great difference."

"That is your great folly. Please me and I'll save your life."

"I can protect myself."

"Ric is a High Priest of Heliopolis, and you're undergoing Grand Bewitchment. You haven't a chance unless I help you." She sat up, reaching her hand out to him.

"I'll give you the counter-magic. I like you, you have an interesting nature."

"Forgive me, Madame Lazare, for beginning something I can't finish." He backed toward the door.

She stretched out on the couch again, stroking her thighs. "I might have saved you."

"I shall send the bald-headed senator to your chamber, madame. You can save him." He reached behind him to the doorknob, not wishing to turn his back on her.

"Send him and twenty more. I want them all in my bed tonight." She reached for her mask, and her blood-red fingernails flickered in the eyeholes, causing the moon-mask to live for a moment, a ruby-eyed monster which said, *Yes, I'm the enchantress, and you are already enchanted, fool.*

H E walked down the long carpeted hallway toward the main staircase. A Florentined door opened beside him, as a servant backed out carrying an empty water bucket.

"Come in!" called Duval. "The Count's bath is big enough for all! Won't you join us?"

Madame Allega, the cabaret star, stood beside the golden tub, dressed as a cabman. The Humble Priest was assisting her out of her costume, and gestured again toward the door. "You aren't coming in? Then you must forgive me . . ." Madame Allega's derrière appeared and Duval gave the door a tap with his foot. "I must baptize this good woman."

Picard continued toward the large staircase. Below, the main room was slowly turning into a shambles, feathers floating in the air, sequins scattering to the floor, other bits of costume coming off. Several of the guests were now sprawled before the great mirror, but there were many still dancing, to music which had grown more sensual, more suggestive, and some of the women had begun interpreting it more boldly. Miss Carter of America was dancing with her two black escorts and her hammock had been taken over by the mad rooster, who swung there supported by his dutiful servants.

Turcotte and Lescadre had absented themselves from the main room. Their principal job, the guarding of the jewels of La Païva, was over. Picard saw her leaving the ballroom with Count von Donnersmarck and the green lizard. He followed them to the front door and watched as they entered their carriage, the most splendid one in the courtyard. When it had glided out between the front gates, he returned to the depths of the house, asked a servant to take him to the cellar, the only avenue of entrance he hadn't secured, and though the rare jewels of La Païva were gone, there was still wealth enough in the ballroom to tempt a thief.

Bearing a lamp, the servant led him down into the large subterranean chambers, and together they examined the small high windows in each room.

"Leave the lamp. I'll remain here awhile."

"Very good, Inspector. There is one more room of furniture and paintings through that doorway. I'll be at the head of the stairs if you require further assistance."

He sat in the gloomy foundation of the mansion, weariness upon him, and a troubling image going round in his brain, of a shadowy figure carrying a knife which gleamed in the darkness of his mind and was gone.

A familiar tiding. When last this shadow appeared to me . . .

Picard entered the final musty room of the cellar, walking slowly through aisles of sheet-covered furniture, piled-up oddities of the Cherubini family, grotesque vases, bizarre washstands and basins.

. . . when last the knife flashed in my brain, it was but one day until Alcide Marusic appeared.

Ten years in prison produces a powerful venom in the veins. Marusic's mouth was practically watering as he came at me. The rue . . . Gabrielle.

And now you've come again, shadow. Is it Lazare you embody, as once before you embodied Marusic, whose blood has long been washed down the gutters of the rue Gabrielle?

The darkness answered with a faint whispering, the sensation of impending danger, of something vicious and cunning advancing against him, advancing slowly across the city, as once Alcide Marusic had advanced with death in his heart. But whereas Marusic had been clumsy, a simple cutthroat mad for revenge, this advancing danger was more clever and more deadly. Picard closed his eyes, trying to feel exactly how he was endangered, and again he heard Lazare's voice in his mind, repeating softly, *It is only a toy, monsieur.*

Very well, Lazare, but you may encounter me sooner than you expected.

Tucked among the Cherubini bric-a-brac and sheeted chairs was an antique bed, a thin muslin canopy surrounding it. Picard parted the veil and entered, crawling onto the bed and closing his eyes. Good wine makes one as sleepy as bad.

The shadowy figure again thrust his knife, parting the way into dreams of blood and glistening steel, where men

long dead danced and gnashed their teeth, flames of hatred
in their eyes.

He woke in darkness; the lamp had burned its oil completely. He groped through the black cellar toward the
stairs. From overhead there came the sound of a few tire-
less masqueraders, but the music had ceased. He climbed
the stairs and walked to the main ballroom.

Count Cherubini, the great rooster, sat in the middle of
the floor, wrapped in a small throw rug, staring into the
deep distances of the mirror. Unconscious beside him on
the floor was Spring, daffodils mostly gone, crocuses
drooping, her bottom bare except for the Count's wine
goblet, which was balanced there. Along the mirror, half-
naked couples were lying on pillows and sofa cushions,
bottles and glasses all around them.

Count Cherubini turned his neck toward Picard. "Has
the sun come up yet?"

"No."

"Would you please alert me the moment the sun starts
to rise? I intend to give a bit of a cock-a-doodle-do."

Picard looked out the window. The sky was still dark,
but he could feel the lateness of the hour in his body. The
Count will not have long to wait.

Inspector Turcotte emerged from the kitchen, guiding
a bird of paradise, who had lost the bottom half of her
costume. As they passed, Turcotte winked at Picard and
tossed him a blue and white feather from his pocket, out
of which numerous other feathers peeked.

The rooster had begun snoring on the floor, his bill rattling with each exhalation. Between snores, faint clucking noises were heard from within his mask, as if he were rehearsing for the dawn.

Of the whores left in the ballroom, none were so great any longer. The great ones had retired earlier, as befitting their stature. Those left at the ball now were perhaps the real whores. Their jewelry was fake; they were covered with little mirrors of glass, which did not sparkle with the intensity of La Païva's gems, and they were not ones to depart a party before dawn; consequently all they were left with were three tired policemen and an unconscious rooster. Lescadre had donned a musketeer's hat and was attending to Spring, who had awakened with a terrible thirst. Lescadre poured champagne into her extended glass. Beside her the rooster continued to snore and squawk softly.

Picard walked through the debris, stopping at the refreshment table to clean up a few dainty sandwiches, swallowing a half-dozen of them quickly. He lifted his mask, placing it on top of his head. A movement at the top of the grand staircase caught his eye. Duval the Humble Priest appeared, two servants behind him, carrying Miss Carter in her hammock. Her hair was dripping wet and her Southern gown was askew. "Please see that Miss Carter is put into a carriage directly," called Duval, coming down the stairs behind them. "She's had a profound religious experience."

Duval spied Picard and came toward him. "My dear Inspector . . . how are you making out with your investigation?"

Picard turned toward the champagne table, not wishing to speak of his work, but Duval babbled on: "You're undoubtedly aware of the latest rumor going around Paris about Lazare."

"His wife bathes in champagne."

"Goat's milk, my dear fellow, I have it on unassailable authority. Will you allow me to give you a lift? I have a carriage waiting."

"I must wake the Count." The courtyard was clearly visible now in the first grey light before dawn. Picard shook the snoring rooster.

"Yes, yes, I'm ready." The rooster rose slowly and stretched his wings, as Picard and Duval helped him to his feet. "Thank you so much. Might I beg your assistance but a few more steps, to the courtyard, please."

They walked down the hall and out, into the courtyard. The rooster shook his comb, bending his head shyly. "I don't feel in the mood for a proper cock-a-doodle."

"Then come with us," said the Humble Priest.

"If it's no intrusion . . . how kind of you." The rooster followed them to Duval's carriage. Duval called to the driver. "Do you know the Hôtel St. Claude?"

The driver lowered his looped whip handle to the door latch and lifted it for the two men and the large barnyard bird.

"A delightful party, my dear Count," said Duval, fingering his rosaries.

"I'm so glad you could come," said the rooster, lighting a slender cigar and putting it to his beak.

Picard stared out the window; the luxurious houses of St. Honoré slipped by slowly.

"I should have brought Spring along," said the rooster. "This is the sort of ride she likes."

"You can find Spring on any street corner in Paris, Count."

"Quite right, dear boy. One forgets . . ." The rooster turned to the window. On the rue de Rivoli, a streetwalker graced the intersection, dressed in black, wearing a high-crowned hat bound with red ribbon.

"Stop the carriage," said the rooster to the cabman, and stepped down as the carriage came to a halt beside the young woman. The rooster stumbled clumsily but was able to regain his balance and give a bow to the lady, his tail feathers raised in the air. "Can we be of assistance, mademoiselle?"

The whore had seen many things on the rue de Rivoli before; but her startled expression indicated that this was the first time she'd seen a six-foot rooster emerge from a carriage shortly before sunrise.

"Don't be alarmed, mademoiselle," said the rooster. "We're only out cock-a-doodling, or preparing to cock-a-doodle, I should say, if we find the proper location. Could you perhaps recommend a suitable site for some enthusiastic crowing?" The rooster scraped completely to the ground, affording her a view of his dangling red crown.

"I can't take you into my room like that," she said, pointing at his feather suit.

"I understand perfectly; perhaps we might walk then, to the riverbank?" He extended his wing and she took it. He waved the other wing at Duval and Picard. "Thank you, gentlemen. Please visit me again . . ."

The driver continued onto St. Antoine. Duval turned to Picard. "Your man Lazare—did you know he operated in Paris once before? At least that's the rumor I've heard." The carriage turned onto the boulevard Beaumarchais.

"How do you suddenly know so much about Lazare?"

"One hears so many stories these days—yes, here we are." The carriage stopped and they stepped down, onto the rue St. Claude. "It was here, Inspector . . ." Duval pointed to the small and darkened windows of the Hôtel St. Claude. "The walls are filled with secret passageways. Do you recall the Affair of the Diamond Necklace?"

"I'm not familiar . . ."

"Inspector, surely you're a historian of crime. A hundred years ago the most famous diamond necklace in the world, destined for the neck of Marie Antoinette, was pinched by the man who lived here, a man certain misty-minded Parisians claim has once again returned to Paris."

"You mean Lazare? That's preposterous."

"Yes, isn't it?" Duval entered the hotel hallway and they walked along it to the staircase. At the foot of the stairs was a statue, a mock copy of an Egyptian pharaoh, holding a lighted gas lamp in his hand. "But of course, Inspector, rumor has it that we're not dealing with an ordinary man, that in fact we're witnessing the game of a man who's discovered the secret of making gold, of causing diamonds to grow bigger, and—" Duval peered up the stairs. "—prolonging life. Absurd, the things people will fall for."

Picard pointed to the plaster pharaoh's head. "It's all done with masks, Duval."

"Yes, masks and mirrors, so they say. He called himself

Grand Cophat of the Masonic Order and Lord of the Egyptian Rite." They turned and walked back down the hallway, to the street, and climbed again into their carriage. "His name was Count Alessandro di Cagliostro."

T H E palaces of the Right Bank were receiving the first rays of dawn. Picard stepped from Duval's carriage, onto the Pont St. Michel. He paused for a moment on the edge of the bridge; from upriver he could hear the faint crowing of a rooster.

Duval leaned his head out the window. "The Count has welcomed the dawn."

Picard turned toward the Prefecture, as Duval's voice called after him: "There's another ball tonight at Madame Valanne's, Inspector! Will we meet there?"

"I've had enough of grand balls."

"Nonsense, Inspector. Eat, drink, and be merry . . ."

The murmuring river completed the ancient phrase, whispering with the voice of his enemy—*Because tomorrow you die*—and again Picard felt himself on the edge of piercing the mirror's secret. He wanted to shatter the jewel of morning, push through to nature's crystalline depths, but he was mortally bound, was woven into the fabric of the sunrise in such a way that he could not escape. And yet he felt that his life depended on penetrating this veil, that he had to gain objectivity—on another star, on some distant point in space, somewhere—in order to outwit the magician who was out to kill him.

He crossed the Pont St. Michel, going toward the Prefecture, where facts prevailed, where the veils of thieves and swindlers were torn aside daily; the good solid walls gave him back his sense of solidarity. Here is my realm, here where I can touch, question, navigate with certainty and bring matters to their logical conclusion. I cannot hope to get behind the secret of the morning, cannot enter the mirror of a glistening river. Such things are for charlatans like Lazare, who use them to mystify others. Whoever enters the mirror is a fool, for he will surely lose his way there. A bit of incense, a turbaned Hindoo, and the doorway to folly is complete. But I am not taken in. This—he knocked on the door of the official records room—this is the only reality.

A sleepy-eyed night clerk admitted him. The records room was musty and stale with the smell of slowly decaying pages, shelf after shelf of them, bound in large leather cases. He scanned the rows, and selected the volume he wanted.

The cases were old, solved, unsolved, having one thing in common—all the participants, criminals and inspectors alike, were now dead. The traitor Chevalier de Rohan, the murderess Madame de Brinvilliers, the elderly musketeer de Creil, who uttered hunting cries in order to disrupt theatrical performances he disliked. Control of the lottery, inspection of the drains, a certain Venetian ambassador and a young actor he admired, their meetings, their quarrel, a cardinal observed entering a brothel where his stay is scrupulously timed; record of search made by Commissioner Chenon, August 23, 1785, by order of the King:

"At seven o'clock in the morning, accompanied by Police Inspector de Brugnières, we went to the rue St. Claude de Marais, to a house called the Hôtel St. Claude, where, having mounted to the first floor and entered an apartment, we found the said Cagliostro in the bedchamber with his wife, Séraphine Feliciani, age twenty-eight."

Cagliostro confined for stealing "the most beautiful diamond necklace in the world," and eventually released, the case against him collapsing and his property returned— large diamond rings, two canes adorned with diamonds, a diamond garter, a ruby cane, diamond pendants and buckles, pearls, garnets, gold boxes, a Chinese inkwell ornamented with gold, gold teaspoons and scissors, and "divers papers." An implicated young woman is branded by the outraged Crown—a fleur-de-lys burned in each of her shoulders.

Picard closed the file and walked down the long echoing hallway. Lazare has copied Cagliostro's style. What worked before can work again. Except that tonight, Lazare, you are out of work for good.

He breakfasted near the Prefecture, eating slowly, reading the newspaper account of Count Cherubini's ball. It was inaccurate, but the young reporter was undoubtedly dazzled by mirrors. As were we all.

Picard checked his pocket watch; the library would soon be opening. He left the café and walked slowly across the Pont des Arts, toward the Quarter. The smells from the bakery shops filled the streets. He passed his ramshackle house and walked on toward St. Germain, thinking of Lazare—a puny fellow, nothing to him at all. Crush his head in my bare hands.

At the rue Bonaparte he turned left, heading for St. Sulpice, which was now bathed in sunlight. The fountain at the center of the square was filled with leaves and rain water, and the sparkling water winked at him, its countless little mirrors promising secrets, if he would look more deeply, look more deeply, dear Inspector, and we will tell you all.

He hesitated at the edge of the fountain, tempted by the dazzling surface, but afraid of its allurement, for already he felt a strange tug inside him, as if there were a fisherman in the depths of the fountain, a fisherman whose mysterious hook had caught his life-force and was pulling on it. His body quivered, fighting the hook. *You're undergoing Grand Bewitchment*, said his opponent's wife softly. He wrenched away from the fountain's edge and walked quietly across the square, toward the library, entered, inquired of the librarian for any material "on a man named Cagliostro."

She returned with a single volume of letters and diary

excerpts compiled by a Dutchman named Van Wamelen, who'd fallen under Cagliostro's spell. The slim little book had been privately printed, done on fine paper and handsomely bound, a token of Van Wamelen's devotion, "to the great master."

Picard carried the book to a table by the window and began reading about the fabulous Grand Cophat of the Masonic Order, Lord of the Egyptian Rite, a sinister and clever imposter who, a hundred years ago, had lied and bluffed his way into the richest salons in Europe. Sorcerer, soothsayer, magician, prophet, gold maker, his rooms at the Hôtel St. Claude had attracted such notable Parisians as General de Labarthe; the General's letters were filled with loyal sentiments toward Cagliostro: "No one's hands are cleaner . . . Mademoiselle Augeard received an elixir from him which caused all her ills to disappear."

Picard went slowly through the praises sung by the noble citizens who had adored Count Cagliostro. They'd all received the elixir of immortality, but were, nonetheless, now among the ranks of the glorious dead, Cagliostro included. Of course, there had sprung up a nitwitted story at the time of his death, that his body had never been seen by anyone but the Pope, who'd had him strangled. "And," wrote Madame Hunziker, "his grave has in fact never been found."

As for Madame Cagliostro, the Duke of Mantinot's diary described her as "more beautiful than any woman I have ever seen. All of Paris draws its breath when she passes on the street . . ."

Picard turned the page and fell into a crevice, into a crack in reality's glass, into the eyes and smile of Madame Cagliostro, whose face was reproduced upon the page. She was the living image of Renée Lazare.

W I T H the morning sun still on him, he sat in the Luxem-
bourg Gardens, looking down toward the pony carts. The
children were taking their rides around the park, dressed
in their wool hats and mittens. Directly in front of him
three other children were inventing an endless game with a
wall, a piece of rope, and a sandpile below. The girl seemed
to be the prize in a struggle between the two boys, but
when she asserted herself too much she was shoved off the
wall into the sand. Her tears did not last long; she
enjoyed the game too much to remain hurt.

His own childhood had been spent in this park, and he
understood its enchantments, knew that this low wall
before him up which the children scrambled was the wall
of a castle, or the Great Wall of China. One of the young
boys now strode along the top, in high boots and a fleece-
lined jacket. He was King, had conquered the sandpile,
the girl, and the other boy, who was heavier and slower.

The girl begged to be hauled up to him by his rope, but he ignored her, staring out over the sprawling garden, his vast domain.

He is like Lazare; fast and arrogant. And I am like this other young lad, slow-moving and bear-like. The heavy boy is gentle with the girl, considerate of her needs. Ah, he loves her, of course.

Picard closed his eyes; Renée Lazare and Madame Cagliostro swam before him, two images that kept becoming one beautiful and incredible female.

Am I to believe that Lazare's elixir of immortality works?

The cries of the young girl brought his eyes open. She'd been tied to a tree. The two boys danced around her, and she hung over the rope, moaning and begging for mercy, which only the heavy boy seemed willing to extend her. His companion in the high boots marched majestically around the captive, scorning her with his eyes.

Picard stood, not wishing to watch any more of the sacrifice, for it had too much the quality of memory, as if he were watching a scene from his own childhood. Though no photograph existed, no little etching of his youthful countenance preserved, he imagined it to be much like this heavyset melancholy boy before him, indeed the child seemed to be himself, forty years ago. I left a piece of my spirit in these gardens, and this lad has taken it, the slow tenderness of my heart.

The boy looked up at Picard, their eyes meeting, and Picard dismissed the exquisite sense that he was seeing himself, that he'd traveled back through time to watch himself. I'm tired, and the weary mind is close to the dreaming mind.

Nonetheless, he gave the fat boy a salute, which the boy answered with quick affection and a shy smile whose gentle radiance reinforced the feeling of time turned inside out, of *déjà vu*, that you and I are one, little bandit, that past, present, and future meet in the morning garden, for purposes known only to the genie.

He felt the boy's eyes still on him as he turned and went along the path. I could tell him that his gentle heart will lead him into one beguilement after another, but he wouldn't understand. His friend, the arrogant one in high boots, he understands. His heart is selfishly his own and will be all his life, and he'll succeed, with politics, women, whatever he turns to.

But what does the genie mean to tell me? Has my heart fallen into some dangerous attraction once again? Is arrogant Lazare bound to succeed against me?

He left the park. He needed sleep. The bread girls were carrying their baskets toward the restaurants and cafés of St. Germain. He shuffled along; a bread girl walked ahead of him, not beautiful, but one of those women who, no matter what they wear, seem to be wearing bedclothes. He suppressed a desire to follow her the length of St. Germain, instead made his way through the streets surrounding the Collège de France, and turned onto St. Jean de Latran, stopping at a large house which smelled of every imaginable filth.

The steps of the wretched cloister were twisted in narrow loops, each landing illuminated by a small broken window. He climbed slowly up the stairs, past the doors of the raucous men and women who lived there—street performers mostly, fire-eaters, sword-swallowers. Their doors were open, their voices filling the halls. The door he sought, however, was tightly closed. He laid his knuckles on it lightly.

He waited, hearing nothing from within, but presently the door opened silently, and an intersection of blackness prevailed at the doorjamb. At belt level a smooth knife blade glistened and then folded itself backward soundlessly.

"Come in, Paul." Albert, the gentle lean-boned thief, smiled and opened the door all the way.

Picard entered the thief's nest, a single room in which there were only two objects—a pile of straw and a nightingale.

"I have to kill someone, before he kills me."

Albert nodded slowly and sat down on the straw, rubbing his face, brushing off sleep. "Who is it?"

"Ric Lazare, the society fortune-teller."

"Why is he after you?"

"I shadowed him and found too much." Picard walked to the window, looked down toward the street.

"Maybe he's bluffing."

"The last fellow who called Lazare's bluff had an ice pick driven through his head."

"Has he hired someone to kill you?"

"I don't know. But I can't afford to wait around and find out."

"Is tonight convenient?"

"Yes. He doesn't retire until very late."

"That's fine. I've got a little job to do first. Can we meet at your place? Around midnight?"

"I'll be there."

Albert got up from the straw mat and padded to the bird cage in his bare feet. "What's his address?"

"Eighty-seven, rue de Richelieu."

"I'll have a look at it this afternoon." Albert opened the nightingale's cage, took the bird out on his finger, and murmured to it lovingly.

Picard turned and went to the door; the hallway received him with its bad smells and rubbish heaps. He was nearly asleep on his feet, and the crisp winter air of the street did nothing to revive him. He headed back toward his own neighborhood, vaguely hoping to meet the bread girl again.

H E rose from a sleep that seemed to have lasted only a moment. Yet it was already dark, the gas lamps lit on the street below, and he was rested, and ferociously hungry; he thought of the Restaurant Widermann, for a meal of grand proportions.

He washed in cold water, dug out his last clean shirt, and transferred his pistol to the hopsack jacket. The Baron's cane called to him as he was tying up his black cravat, and he believed in listening to his weapons when they spoke, for they too had a fate to fulfill, and who knows, slender friend, perhaps you will be the instrument of Lazare's demise. One thing is certain, it happens tonight.

He took his top hat, his gloves, extinguished the light, and descended the stairs. A winter wind had begun to blow off the river. He hailed a carriage and sank into its cold cushions. I must contain myself to some degree at this restaurant and not eat myself into extinction. There's work to do tonight. I'll avoid the cabbage steeped in ten layers of lard.

He ate enthusiastically, but did not fully abandon himself, as was his custom with Herr Widermann's cuisine. Indeed he felt his new resolution taking firm hold in him, to always eat this way, less like a savage and more like a sage. When it was time to order dessert, he bypassed the enormous and delightful apricot *Knödel*, settling for a humbler dish of almonds, wine, and currants.

Nonetheless, he was forced to unbutton his jacket, and in doing so slipped his hand to the leather pouch inside, touching the handle of his revolver for luck. Ten grains of black powder in each cartridge, Lazare. You'll laugh out of the other side of your mouth tonight. You'll die laughing in your bed.

He rose, and took his cape from the attendant near the door.

"And your gloves, sir."

He slipped his hands into the fine leather, made specially thin for men who bear arms. Conflicting in no way with the quick firing of a pistol, Monsieur Lazare, as Baron Mantes will testify to when you meet in hell.

He stepped onto the boulevard Bonne Nouvelle. Men's lives are cheap: thousands, millions, billions, gone, gone. One more going tonight.

On the boulevard du Temple he paused before the windows of the old clothes shop, but the windows were dark, casting no reflection. I've killed men and it changes nothing. They don't creep around my bed at night.

The sound of circus music drew him on, the rolling of

drums, the blare of trumpets. The doors of the Cirque d'Hiver promised "Equestrian Performances, Accompanied by Acrobatic Feats, Pantomime, Etc." He looked at his watch; until midnight, then.

The red gates admitted him, and he passed beneath the carved golden horses, going into the crowded auditorium. The magic of the place took him immediately—the smell of the African animals, a bareback-riding girl in spangled red tights, dark-haired; her heavy thighs and muscular calves were formidable, charming.

As she rode past him, he saw that the smile was frozen on her face and her eyes didn't blink. Completely concentrated. Would make a fine killer. And what are all these society women doing here tonight?

He moved his eyes slowly along the front row of the audience; the gowns were expensive, and the faces were not those usually seen at the circus, were rather the sort one saw in the box seats at the opera, the concert hall—Princesse Mathilde, Mademoiselle de Galbois, Princesse d'Essling.

". . . from the Persian Gulf, ladies and gentlemen, we are proud to present the Strongest Man in the World—the Great Harid!"

A ferocious-looking thug stepped into the ring. His dark greasy hair and olive skin gave him an exotic appearance, but his tattooed arms contained the usual ships, anchors, and indecent phrases of the common French sailor. Picard leaned against the railing of the arena and watched the strong man pick up a hundred-pound horse weight in his teeth and fling it over his head; it descended with a loud crash onto a metal plate laid on the floor.

Princesse Mathilde gasped, applauded, and the Great Harid looked at her with scornful lust in his eyes.

"Now the Great Harid will lift ten men! Ten men! May we please have volunteers . . ."

Picard stepped aside as the gate to the ring was opened and the volunteers passed through, ten men who climbed on a board suspended between two wooden blocks. The Great Harid stooped beneath the board, brought his shoulders up to it, and lifted men and board up and down, and up again, as if it were all no more than a sack of potatoes. Mademoiselle de Galbois squealed with delight and once again the Strongest Man in the World bowed to the court ladies, with a look that said he would lift them up too, if they so desired, on the end of his prick.

". . . and now the Great Harid will lift an elephant!"

The trumpets sounded, and a baby elephant came lumbering forth, to whom the roustabouts attached a set of chains leading upward to a metal platform. The Great Harid climbed to the top of the platform, put his body into a harness attached to the chains, and proceeded to lift the elephant two feet off the floor, where it swung back and forth.

"The Great Harid, ladies and gentlemen!"

Harid bowed for the last time, his greasy hair hanging over his shoulders, his eyes lasciviously bright.

"And now, ladies and gentlemen—" The ringmaster cracked his whip. "—our magnificent master of the high wire—Léotard!"

A young mustachioed man in black tights came bounding out, climbed up the ropes like a monkey, and swung on a trapeze, flying from it to another one across the arena, leaping about, slipping forward over the depths. He spun, he sailed, drew shrieks of terror from the ladies, and when he finally descended the guide rope the ringmaster announced that photos of the Great Léotard in thirty-five aerial poses were available in the lobby.

The handsome young acrobat walked around the ring, bowing this way and that, and then spying some friends in the audience he made his way to the edge of the ring and called the ringmaster over to him. Snapping his whip nervously, the ringmaster walked with a brisk militaristic stride to where Léotard stood. The audience craned their necks, trying to see whom he'd singled out, and the ringmaster, after conferring with Léotard for a moment, satisfied everyone's curiosity with an announcement:

"Ladies and gentlemen, Léotard has informed us that two great circus performers are with us tonight, colleagues of his from early days of adventure on the high wire. They are two people you have all read of, the couple who have become the sensation of all Paris, the dazzling, the fabulous—Ric and Renée Lazare!"

Picard moved slowly around the arena, trying to mask the excitement in his body as he fixed his eyes on Lazare's heart and quickly removed the rubber tip from the pistol-cane. Perfectly accurate at thirty yards. A quick flick of the wrist is all that's necessary. Lazare will fall, as I merge with the crowd. Fate leads me to you, Lazare, the wandering night has its own design, and you and I are appointed to meet in a puff of smoke, which will be gone in an instant, and so will I be gone, along that railing, and out that doorway.

The ringmaster was between him and Lazare, beginning another announcement, cracking his whip again for attention. "Léotard has persuaded his friends to perform for us, ladies and gentlemen, in a rare exhibition of high-wire excellence. Give them just a moment, please, to change into suitable costume . . ." The ringmaster and Léotard flanked Ric and Renée Lazare as they descended to the ring, and Léotard showed them toward the dressing room.

". . . In the meantime, while we're waiting for our brave couple to rejoin us, I am happy to present to you the world-renowned Nadine Hatto and her performing doves!"

Picard took a seat near the dressing-room door, and watched the bird woman bring doves out of her sleeves, out of an assortment of empty boxes, after which she made them disappear into her handkerchief and into thin air. The doves, ragged-looking from being stuffed into one small escape hatch after another, were faithful and intelligent. They landed on Nadine's shoulders, on her head, on her arms, and at the end of the performance she was covered with white doves, and walked out with them all over her, as Ric and Renée Lazare made their entrance.

Lazare wore white satin trunks, studded with jewels in arabesque shape. His sleeveless shirt was also white and similarly adorned; his slim muscular body looked as comfortable in the circus ring as it did in the salon. Renée was in black, her brief costume clinging to her with revealing tightness. Her long hair was tied up in a severe chignon and she climbed the guide rope with quick, sure strength, Lazare following her.

The society ladies in the front row were standing, as the Lazares stood upon the trapeze platform, accepting their applause. The drums rolled again and Ric Lazare untied the trapeze bar and swung out in the air. Picard cocked the hammer on his pistol-cane. You're a fine and talented lad, Lazare, and you're going to die in style.

Lazare spun on the trapeze bar, releasing it for a moment and sliding down it, hooking it at the last moment with his feet. The audience cheered and he bent himself back up to the bar, swinging with it to the opposite platform, where he landed gracefully, still clutching the bar.

With the applause ringing out, and the drums rolling, Renée Lazare swung into the air, back and forth, gaining altitude. Again the trumpets sounded and Ric Lazare swung from his side of the ring. She released herself from her bar and floated toward him. Their hands met in the air, wrists locking.

Picard stood, watching the two graceful beings above him, as they sailed over the heads of the crowd, riding the bar together, their right arms outstretched in triumph.

The whole of Paris is theirs now. They've captured everyone from the Emperor to the ice-cream vendor. Captured all hearts but one, and mine they shall never capture.

For I'm like the Great Harid—a hulking brute who can never enjoy the finesse of the heights. Harid and I remain below, in the sawdust, while you, monsieur and madame, climb to the clouds. I should like to try and lift that elephant. Steady now, here's the moving target.

They descended the guide rope, gliding down and leaping to the center of the ring as the crowd rose to its feet, applauding wildly. Picard edged forward, closer to the dressing-room door. The noise will not be heard. The crowd will only see Lazare clutch his chest and sink to the floor. All eyes will be on him.

Ric and Renée Lazare were approaching slowly, smiling at the crowd and waving to their friends. The ringmaster cracked his whip and three clowns rushed into the arena, a whirlwind of rags and flapping shoes. Picard took one step closer as Ric Lazare came into range. And now, Lazare, you die . . .

"Oh, monsieur, it is you! I'm so grateful . . ."

A hand clutched his arm, and he found himself suddenly embraced by a young woman. Desperately he struggled with his cane, trying to turn and fire, but the young woman thrust her face before him, blocking his view completely.

"Do you recognize me, monsieur? You saved my life in Nuremberg. He was a murderer, as you said, the man you shot down at the skating rink. I'm so grateful—we're visiting Paris, my family and I. You must meet them, they will be so pleased. I never thought I'd see you again . . ."

Picard craned his neck, trying to find Lazare's back, but a clown jumped in front of him.

"You're dead!" shouted the clown, firing a small rubber ball from the end of his popgun. It sailed toward Picard and struck him lightly on the forehead, then recoiled on the end of a string, as Ric and Renée Lazare passed out of sight into the dressing room.

FROM the trunk of the solitary tree that graced the rue de Nesle, a shadow disengaged itself and Albert came forward soundlessly. Picard met him at the curb. "Were you waiting long?"

"I enjoy waiting," said Albert. "I listen to the houses."

"They talk to you?"

"The stairs, the windows, the doors—always."

Picard led the way through the hall of his building. From within the concierge's room low voices came, calling the cards. The cat jumped on the staircase. They climbed to Picard's floor, and he opened the door to his apartment. "We have a brief wait . . . I have some food." He lit the lamp on the living-room wall, where the little acrobat still hung, caught in the holy thread.

"You're collecting toys?"

"Yes," said Picard, turning to Albert, in order to show him the hanging acrobat more closely. But Albert was staring at another toy, upon the living-room table, a toy of the same size as the acrobat but with a different costume and a different face. The costume was evening wear—top hat and cloak. The face . . .

"A perfect likeness of you," said Albert. "Where did you pose for it?"

Picard went to it slowly and picked it up. The workmanship was extraordinary, as if made by elves, by tiny carpenters and tailors. But he wasn't charmed.

The toys can work evil . . . The voice of Appel Meisterlin came to him as he held the miniature being in his hand, and his heart was racing.

"Does it move about?" asked Albert, in a voice from childhood, fascinated, hopeful.

"I expect it does," said Picard, handing it to Albert, his hand faintly trembling.

"There must be a key . . ." Albert investigated beneath the cloak.

"In the back," said Picard. "There should be a key in the back . . ." Just a toy. Nothing more than a toy.

"No, there's no key . . . wait a moment, I've got it." A clicking sound drew Picard back to the toy. Albert was turning the head around and around. "Here's the key—the whole head. Like wringing someone's neck."

Albert set the miniature Inspector on the table; the toy walked forward slowly, like a bear, then toppled over on the tablecloth, the legs kicking clumsily in the air.

"Imperfectly balanced," said Albert. "Still, what a remarkable resemblance."

The key unwound and the tiny Inspector Picard lay still, face down on the table. Picard picked it up, then went to the wall and took down the hanging acrobat. He

carried both of them to the kitchen and threw them into
the coal stove. The tiny figures lay unmoving on the
smoldering bed, as their clothes caught fire. Then the
acrobat jumped, his spring expanding in the heat, jumped
and tumbled on the flames which rose up as Picard opened
the draft on the stove.

His toys, said Appel Meisterlin, *had little souls.*

The top-hatted toy, the miniature Picard, kicked its
legs and rolled slowly over as the flames devoured its
body. A sound of springs echoed in the hollow chamber
of the stove, the metal cries of the little creatures in their
death anguish. Picard tossed a few coals on top of them
and closed the stove.

He slid a pan over the heat and sliced in vegetables and
a piece of fish. Albert joined him at the stove as the food
sizzled. The thief took a newspaper from his pocket and
handed it to Picard, pointing at a column in the center
of the page:

PROWLER IN PALACE

*Monsieur Hyrvoix, Chief of the Palace Guard, said that
a prowler entered the Palace last night, avoiding capture
and making his way through many of the Imperial rooms.
According to Hyrvoix, nothing was stolen, but an officer
of the Elite Cavalry Corps was knocked unconscious. It is
believed the prowler was an Italian spy. Entrance was made
through the cellar. Hyrvoix has called for additional guards-
men and renewed vigilance during this time of political
tension . . .*

Picard handed the paper back to Albert. "You?"

Albert opened his shirt collar and withdrew a gold

chain from around his neck. On the end of it dangled a dark dried piece of wood.

"The True Cross?"

"I replaced it with a perfect replica. No one will ever know the difference."

"You said you had a buyer . . ."

"I was to have met one of the Pope's emissaries today, but I've decided to keep it for a while." Albert took the chain back from Picard and put it around his neck. "If it is the True Cross, what power is in it."

"Do you feel any different wearing it?"

"Not at all."

Picard laid out two plates and slid the sautéed food onto them.

They took to the street together, going slowly, allowing time for Paris to pass into its slumber. Lazare has been on the high wire; he must be tired now, tired and drifting into sleep. Sleep, Lazare, sleep deeply. Have beautiful dreams.

The Seine flowed peacefully; the night was windless and still. They walked beneath the lamplight of the bridge, their shadows long and their footsteps silent. "There are others in his house—servants—I would rather not hurt them."

"At most," said Albert, bringing a leather-covered blackjack from his pocket, "a rap on the head."

They left the bridge and walked along the rue du Pont-Neuf. At the intersection ahead of them a peculiarly rotund figure appeared, stepping from the doorway of a townhouse on the rue de Rivoli.

"It's Count Cherubini," said Picard.

"Why is he wearing a barrel?"

"He's been to a costume ball."

The Count weaved drunkenly to the curb. His torso was clad in a large wine barrel, on which was lettered:

Perrier Jouët
1857

The rest of his body was outfitted in evening clothes. Picard and Albert approached him, as he fumbled in the gutter.

"Are you in need of assistance, Count?"

Cherubini turned toward them, his eyes glazed, but friendly. "How kind of you. I'm attempting to get the spigot open on my barrel. It seems to have jammed."

"We need a glass," said Albert, kneeling by the spigot and removing a small wrench from his sash of burglar tools.

"Yes," said Cherubini. "There's a glass on the way. The gentleman in the hall . . ." He pointed toward the mansion. The door opened and Duval appeared in his monk's robe, carrying an empty wine glass. He saw Picard and smiled.

"Inspector—glad you could make it. Is the wine flowing, Count?" Duval stepped to the barrel.

"It will flow now," said Albert, turning the spigot as Duval placed the glass underneath it.

"An excellent year," said the Count. "One of the very best."

Albert turned off the spigot and Duval held out the filled glass to Cherubini. "I'll go for more glasses," said the Humble Priest, returning to the doorway of the mansion.

"He's an excellent fellow," said the Count. "Right there when you need him."

Other revelers looked out from the front windows of the house. Albert replaced the burglar tool inside his sash. Duval came back, bearing three more glasses. Picard worked the spigot and the wine flowed. They held their glasses up.

"Cheers, my dear fellows."

"Your health, Count."

The delicate rims clicked lightly in the still night air.

"Shall we have another?" asked the Humble Priest, bending toward the barrel.

"Please, let's drink it all," said the Count. "It will make walking lighter."

The glasses were passed beneath the spigot once again. Count Cherubini sipped the vintage wine, turned toward the townhouse. "Madame Valanne—do you know Madame Valanne?—she objected to my barrel. Refused to have it in bed with her."

"The hell with her," said Albert, draining his glass.

"Exactly," said the Count.

"Go to this address," said Albert, scribbling on a card. "Ask to see Monique."

"Oh, splendid," said the Count, taking the card. "She won't object to . . ." He pointed at his barrel.

"She'll love it."

"I'm so glad," said the Count. "I do like an effective costume."

"We must go," said Picard.

"Gentlemen, a last toast," said Cherubini.

"To Monique."

"Her health, her prosperity."

The glasses were emptied and Picard and Albert handed theirs to Duval, who tucked them into his robe. Cherubini stepped into the street, hailing a carriage, and Duval opened the door for him, but the Count's barrel would not fit through it. Duval climbed in ahead and pulled at the Count's arms, while Picard and Albert pushed from behind, finally popping Cherubini into the coach. The Count called Monique's address to the cabman and the carriage pulled away. Cherubini opened the window, waving. "Gentlemen, the best to you . . . come visit me . . . anytime . . . *addìo!*"

The carriage rumbled down Rivoli and turned toward the river, as Picard and Albert headed toward Richelieu.

"A splendid wine."

"The Count only drinks the best," said Picard. His spirit was bubbling from the rare vintage, and he was eager to complete the night's work. They walked along, their shadows the only other figures on the street. It was the hour of night he knew best, when most of Paris sleeps and the underworld makes its move. Tonight I move with them.

"I must kill him, you understand?"

"I shall be no more than your second," said Albert.

They passed the Imperial Palace. The courtyard was brightly lit but the rooms of the Palace were mostly darkened. They turned onto Richelieu, passing the first few shops of the street. "My hatter." Picard pointed to a dark shopwindow, where various top hats were displayed on faceless wooden heads.

They stopped and studied the silk hats. "He's slightly mad," said Picard. "Claims that any man who wears his hats will gain distinction in the world."

"And you—"

"I'm proof that he is wrong. But I'll tell you this—the wind will not blow my hat off. It fits that well."

They continued up the street, leaving the shops behind. The townhouses were darkened, the courtyards empty. The black iron gatework outside the Lazare mansion was high, and the gate itself was locked. Albert nodded toward the end of the block. "There's a passage that connects to his garden. We climb the wall and we're in."

They walked on past the Lazare residence, into a cobblestone lane. On both sides of them were stables; the horses could be heard within, breathing in their sleep, stamping their hooves through galloping dreams. The lane smelled of their sweet hay and manure, and was completely dark. Lazare's back wall formed the dead end of the lane. Albert scaled the wall, flattening himself upon it and surveying the garden. Then he was gone down the other side, dropping soundlessly to the ground.

Picard reached up, hauling himself to the top. The bear is known to climb on occasion—he dropped to the ground beside Albert—when he is hungry enough.

The ground was frozen, left no tracks as they crossed the garden to the back door. Albert knelt before it, closely examining the lock. He removed a long wire from his tool sash and slid it through the lock, his actions so silent that Picard thought for a moment he was going deaf. The lock yielded and they entered the darkened house. Albert lit a match. They were in a pantry off the kitchen. He led them forward through the kitchen and into a service hall on the main floor. The smell of flowers filled the air, growing stronger as they stepped into the parlor.

Plants and vines hung in the moonlit windows, the night-blooming narcissus pouring its fragrance through the room. But where the fabulous guests had stood and whispered of their fate and fortune, there was only the carpet of Persia, its minarets and spires muffling all sound of footsteps now, as Albert pocketed a gold inkwell.

The long-dead report of Inspector de Brugnières flashed in Picard's mind: . . . *a Chinese inkwell, ornamented with gold . . . returned to the said Cagliostro when sufficient evidence could not be found to hold him in custody . . .*

Cagliostro or Lazare, whichever you are, your hour has come. Picard moved with Albert across the moonlit rug, to the outer hall and the bottom of the staircase.

A sudden flash of light on the landing above sent them into the shadows beneath the stairs. Soft footsteps descended, accompanied by a candle flame.

A woman paused at the base of the stairs, directly before their hiding eyes. Her skin was milk-white, her hair blazing red, and she was magnificent, standing with a nobility which was intensified by the beauty of her dark robe and the candlelight in her dark close-set eyes. Lazare was close beside her, and they whispered in soft fluent Spanish, its sensuous rhythms expressing a strange passion between them. She gestured with her black gloves, as if presenting Lazare with a great gift, which he accepted with his cold glittering stare.

Then the woman was quickly gone along the outer hall, and Lazare closed the door behind her, his footsteps moving off toward the west wing of the house and fading into silence.

"*Was it she?*" whispered Albert.

"*Yes*," answered Picard, as they stepped out from under the staircase.

"*Long live the Empress*," said Albert with a leering smile. He stuck his tongue out and opened his mouth like a mad ape, licking the air through which she'd passed, as if tasting some last trailing bit of her radiance.

Picard moved up the hallway. Lazare had made no further sound. Somewhere in the west wing . . .

They glided through the dark hallway, toward the front rooms of the mansion. Upon the wall was a large painting of a serpent, rearing on its tail, an arrow through its throat. Albert stopped to peer at it, as they listened to the house, hearing only an impenetrable stillness.

Then Albert moved quickly to a dark wooden door which opened soundlessly to his touch; the thief seemed now to be all shadow, his body swallowed in some profoundly concentrated move, which Picard attempted to match as they stepped into Lazare's workshop.

Upon the wall was a rack of carefully hung tools; the bench beneath it was filled with tiny gear wheels and springs. A single candle glowed on the bench, illuminating the faces of several completed toys—a Spanish dancing girl with the face of Empress Eugénie, a springing tiger, a circus acrobat with the heroic stance and features of the daring Léotard. These and others lined the shelves on every side.

Albert brought the candle toward a display table, on which a miniature army was arranged, with cannon and musket, dressed in the uniform of Prussia. The cavalry was in close formation on both flanks and the officers were leading the charge. Picard moved toward the table.

"*Fire!*" said a tiny voice, no louder than the vibrating of a hair.

The cannons exploded and Picard reeled backward in pain, a shell bursting into his stomach, burying back in his guts.

"*Fire!*" cried the little voice again, joined by others, many others, one after another, as Picard sank to the floor, bullets tearing at his chest and neck.

He saw Albert twist crazily and fall. The thief sprawled beside him, a bullet hole in the center of his forehead, sightless eyes still open in amazement.

"*Fire! Fire! Fire!*"

The room was filled with smoke, the powerful little cannon-pistols raking the air. Waistcoat soaked with blood, Picard crawled toward the table from which the tiny army was firing and pushed himself beneath it, into the maze of wires which controlled the cannons. The wires contracted into the adjacent wall and the cannons sent forth another volley, triggered by an enemy hidden somewhere beyond the wall.

Picard rose up, lifting the table on his massive shoulders, tearing the wires loose from the wall, silencing the guns. He staggered in the acrid smoke, the table on his back, the weight tremendous, like an elephant, like the world itself, impossible to carry, but he struggled with it, knowing he had to carry it forever.

"*. . . ladies and gentlemen, the Great Harid!*"

The crowd roared. The roaring grew louder, so loud he couldn't stand it, a deafening roar in his ears, in his brain, in his whole body.

He collapsed, spilling the toy army onto the floor.

Blood gushed from his wounds, forming a pool all around him, and he lay staring into the eyes of a little artillery officer. The details of the uniform were perfect. The face was that of Ric Lazare.

Picard sighed, his whole body heaving forward and then freezing.

Death tore him violently out of his body and wrenched him upward in a single powerful leap. An immense thunderclap sounded and Paris was below, a vapor, a chimera. Death bowed and swiftly departed, his errand complete.

Dead, dead, dead, echoed the wind as Picard struggled against the threads which were lifting him, up out of the earth's sparkling theatre, reeling him upward through the dark sky. He struggled, but his strength was nothing against the fine golden line.

A terrible wind whirled him higher, whipping the golden threads, and he dangled like an empty costume flapping in the air.

Golden threads were shining everywhere, billions of them, undulating, never tangling, connected to the earth below and controlled by secret mastery from above, whose power now reeled him faster, until he was a comet speeding upward through the heavens.

He resisted, forced a turning in the threads and looked downward at the earth—a small blue ornament in space, one of a little cluster of ornaments around the sun. Then the brilliant sun and its cluster dropped away, becoming no more than a tiny light among countless others.

Desperately he searched for a prayer, but his lips were sealed, sewn with golden thread. Overhead he saw the dome of existence, a curving transparency on which the lights of the universe were reflected. He struck against the dome and passed through it, into utter darkness. He was alone and the universe was below him—a great star-filled ball.

A bell rang.

"Your twenty-five seconds are up, Monsieur Fanjoy," said the butler softly, opening the door of the chamber.

Picard spun around, and the white-turbaned Hindoo bowed to him, his eyes shining darkly, a faint smile on his face.

The telegraph machine clicked, and the Hindoo handed a slip of paper to Picard, who opened it with shaking hands and read the words:

FATA MORGANA

"If you'll step this way, please . . ." The butler's voice was more insistent now and Picard let it carry him out of the room.

He went down the long hallway slowly, as if he were emerging from the land of the pharaohs, from the darkness of a gigantic tomb. His footsteps echoed behind the butler's, and he listened with all his heart, trusting in the echoing hallway as the only certain reality.

"Monsieur Fanjoy—" The butler bowed quietly again, admitting Picard back into the Lazare parlor, where the guests looked at him, indirectly, casually, but knowing that he had undoubtedly received a strange and perhaps shattering message.

The candles in the chandeliers blazed with peculiar

intensity, and the green vines and tendrils which surrounded the Grecian columns were the most comforting
sight he'd ever seen. With trembling steps he walked
toward Ric Lazare.

Lazare was smiling faintly, as had the Hindoo. "Well,
Inspector?"

Picard stared into the uncanny eyes of Lazare, seeing in
them all that he'd seen in the crystal ball—the young
acrobat, the toy maker of Deep Sorrow, the murderer of
Anton Romani. You are the rarest killer in the world and
only a fool would oppose you. "Good night, monsieur."

The small clique at the doorway parted for Picard as
he passed out of the parlor, into the entrance hall. A footman awaited him at the cloakroom, producing his cape
and gloves. He slipped into them quickly, heard footsteps
behind him, and turned. Duval was coming down the hallway toward him, and they stepped together into the
courtyard. It was wrapped in fog, a light drizzle falling,
the rain-mist mingling with the sudden tears that filled
his eyes. Alive!

He twirled his cane, Duval chattering beside him, his
voice the echo of a thousand infinitudes of night.

"Inspector? Did I hear him address you as a police
inspector?"

"Yes," said Picard. "So watch your step, Duval."

"No one's to be trusted these days," sighed Duval, as
they walked through the iron gate to the rue de Richelieu.
Duval hailed a carriage. "Can I leave you anywhere, Inspector?"

Picard called to the driver. "Do you know the Café
Orient?"

"Pigalle," nodded the driver.

Picard climbed in beside Duval and the carriage started forward, into the rue Drouot.

"A most enlightening evening," said Duval. "I must get myself a suite of rooms and a crystal ball. You have to be in front with something original these days." He turned to Picard. "You look quite pale, Inspector. Did Lazare's machine tell you something disturbing?"

The carriage turned onto the rue Notre Dame de Lorette. The lights of Pigalle winked in the distance. Picard sat in silence, his eyes fixed on the lights.

"I hope you don't mind my asking," said Duval. "One is naturally curious. Did it involve—a woman, perhaps?"

Picard stared out the window. "As a matter of fact, it did." He watched as the carriage rolled quickly along, and the glittering lights of the cafés came closer. Amongst them he could already pick out the Café Orient, the coiling dragons glittering on its glass doorway.

"Here you are, monsieur," called the driver, bringing the carriage to the curb.

"Do you see her there, Inspector?" asked Duval, following the look in Picard's eyes.

"I believe so," said Picard, opening the carriage door.

"Well, Inspector, remember—Eldorado Investments—"

Picard walked through the fine drizzle toward the café and entered, crossing the terrace toward the brunette in mauve.

"Good evening," he said, seating himself at her table.

"Why do you look at me so strangely?" she asked, with a smile, her earrings tinkling as she moved her head.

"Because you're so lovely," said Picard, lighting the candle on the table, the dancing little flame causing her eyes to glow. He reached into his pocket, took out the bit of telegraph paper and held it in the flame.

"A love letter?" she asked, watching it curl and burn.

"An affair best forgotten," said Picard.

In the distance, from the station at the Place Roubaix, he heard the whistle of a train.

But in Nuremberg, a few days hence, at a skating rink in the moonlight—

You and I, my dear Baron, shall meet again.

A Note on the Type

The text of this book was set on the Linotype in Janson, a recutting made direct from type cast from matrices long thought to have been made by the Dutchman Anton Janson, who was a practicing type founder in Leipzig during the years 1668–87. However, it has been conclusively demonstrated that these types are actually the work of Nicholas Kis (1650–1702), a Hungarian, who most probably learned his trade from the master Dutch type founder Dirk Voskens. The type is an excellent example of the influential and sturdy Dutch types that prevailed in England up to the time William Caslon developed his own incomparable designs from them.

Composed by The Maryland Linotype Composition Company, Inc., Baltimore, Maryland. Printed and bound by The Haddon Craftsmen, Inc., Scranton, Pennsylvania.

Illustrations by Joe Servello
Typography and binding design by
Margaret McCutcheon Wagner